Holidays After Dark

WINTER'S EVE

VALENTINE'S ARROW

FIREWORKS IN THE BAYOU

SNOWFLAKES AND VAMPIRE KISSES

ASTRID VAIL

Cover Art by Artscandare Design

Edited by NiceGirlNaughtyEdits

First Edition: August 2024

ISBN

Paperback: 978-1-958641-40-8

Broad Content warning includes spicy on page sex scenes and adult language.

This author does not use AI in their writing or cover art.

Contents

Blurb & Content Warning

Holidays After Dark Omnibus features four romantic fantasy and paranormal romance short stories centered around the holidays.

Included in the following pages are:

Winter's Eve: A M/F Winter Fantasy Romance Short Story

Valentine's Arrow: A M/F Valentine's Day Paranormal Romance Short Story

Fireworks in the Bayou: A M/F Fourth of July Paranormal Romance Short Story

Snowflakes and Vampire Kisses: A M/F Paranormal Romance Christmas Short Story

Blurbs and content warnings specific to each story are included before each short story starts.

This book is intended for mature readers only.

Broad content warning as follows:

HOLIDAYS AFTER DARK

Adult language & on page sex scenes

Winter's Eve

Holidays After Dark

Astrid Vail

Blurb and Content Warning

Winter's Eve: An Erotic M/F Holiday Short Story

Beatrix Claus is the new Santa and more than happy to take over the family business.

Except she is already failing as Christmas Eve fast approaches.

Her magical sleigh is on the fritz, and she has no intention of begging the son of Krampus to help her. She would rather prance around naked and summon the fabled Reindeer King.

Only he isn't a fable, and the Reindeer King is happy to help his new Santa in more ways than one.

Content Warning: Adult language, explicit sex scenes, miscommunication, and relocation.

Chapter One

"CANDY CANE COCKSUCKER!" BEATRIX'S voice rang out though the old two-story stables. She rolled out from under the hunk of junk that was supposed to be her sleigh and narrowed her eyes at the frowning elf. "What?" she sneered.

The elf rolled her eyes and handed Beatrix a wrench. "You are the new Santa, Beatrix. And I, for one, did not help raise such a lady with that type of mouth."

This time, Beatrix rolled her eyes and scooted back under the mechanical sleigh. Gone were the old days when Santa delivered presents all over the world with a sleigh pulled by reindeer. Beatrix sighed and hooked the wrench onto an oil-slicked lug nut. The damn sleigh was more finicky than anything else that operated at the North Pole. And while Beatrix was usually a master at fixing anything mechanical, this sleigh was truly something else.

She was just about to give up when the wrench finally moved. "Fuck y—" Oil sprayed all over Beatrix's face and she shrieked in anger. "I'm done! You are a fucking hunk of junk." She rolled out from under the sleigh and stalked away, pointing at the disapproving elf on the way. "Don't you even start." The elf shook her head and sighed before pulling out her phone. Beatrix's eyes narrowed. "Just who do you think you are calling?"

The elf smiled and held up the phone, which Beatrix took gently, trying not to get too much oil on it. She could see the small picture of herself, her blonde hair sticking up from her haphazardly made bun and half of her face covered with oil. Her red jumpsuit looked worse for wear, and she inwardly winced when the video call picked up. A sun-kissed face with rosy cheeks and perfectly curled snow-white hair frowned at her. "Trix, honey, what is all over your face? Why are you so dirty? Hold on, let me get your father."

Beatrix's mother frowned at her through the phone and tossed it down onto whatever chair she had vacated. Beatrix squinted and took in the bright blue sky overhead, along with the sound of water lapping against something. She waited impatiently for her mother to get back and tapped her black snow boot on the ground. After a moment, Beatrix realized she was tapping out the tune to a Christmas song and stopped immediately. She might be the new Santa Claus, but that didn't mean she had to live and breathe Christmas.

A rustle from the phone caught her attention, and she smiled at the new face. Her father smiled back through his massive white beard. "Trix, honey, what seems to be the matter? Is everything going well at the North Pole?"

Beatrix sighed and nodded. "Everything is fine. I don't know why Megi called you. She is just worried about nothing."

"The sleigh is broken!" Megi's shrill voice rang out, and Beatrix's father frowned.

"Honey, that doesn't sound like nothing. We should come back. Is it the magic, or is it something mechanical?"

Beatrix shook her head. "Absolutely not. You and Mom both need this vacation. You have run Christmas for the two hundred and thirty years. It is my turn now. Now tell Mom I said—"

"You are not getting away that quickly, Trix. You didn't answer my question."

Beatrix groaned and pinched at the bridge of her nose. "It's mechanical."

Her father smiled. "You had me worried for a moment! If it is mechanical, then you can get it fixed easy enough before Christmas Eve. I'll tell your mother you love her, and we will see you come the new year."

He hung up quickly, and Beatrix slapped the phone back into Megi's waiting hand. "You lied," she squeaked out.

"It's no big deal. I'll get the stupid thing working again." Beatrix turned on her heel and stalked over to the giant sink perched on the wall next to a stack of glistening harnesses. Harnesses that haven't been used in over four hundred years. They still gleamed after all this time; wild magic embedded into them. Too bad Beatrix didn't have access to *that* type of magic. Megi frowned at Beatrix as she scrubbed at her face, trying to get all the grease and oil off. She turned off the faucet once Megi started tapping her foot. "Fine, Megi. What is your solution, then? I know it's not mechanical, even as much as I wish it was. It's the magic. It is waning. What would you have me do?"

Megi held up the phone. "You need to call him and make amends."

Beatrix laughed. "I would rather prance my naked ass all over the tundra and sleep with the Reindeer King, then talk to *him* again."

Megi gasped and slapped the phone across Beatrix's thigh. "Don't you dare utter those words. Not in this place and not at this time of the year."

Beatrix grinned and took a step away, hands raised. "Reindeer King."

Megi scowled, taking a step forward for every step Beatrix took back. "Don't, Beatrix."

"Ohhhhh, Reindeer Kinggggg!" she sang. "Reindeer King, I am waiting for youuuuu. Come and steal me away."

Megi shook her head, her exasperated sigh sounding more like a squeak. "Girl, what am I supposed to do with you?"

Beatrix shrugged and headed toward the large stable doors. "Come on, Megi. It's a joke. I know the Reindeer King no longer exists. Or else we wouldn't be in this mess to begin with." She motioned to the sleigh.

Megi gave her a quizzical look before motioning to the door. "That is enough for today. You still have lists to double check. Why don't we go inside, and I'll make you some hot cocoa."

Beatrix smiled and opened the door for Megi. "Now that sounds like an excellent plan."

Chapter Two

"I TAKE IT BACK. This was a horrible idea. Is this list *growing*?" Beatrix's bewilderment cut through her annoyance. "It *is* growing. Look. Look!" She shoved the paper in Megi's direction and stabbed at the newest name. "How am I supposed to check this list if it keeps changing?"

Megi scooted a mug of hot cocoa in her direction, topped with mini marshmallows and a candy cane stick. Beatrix moved it to the side and glared at the elf. "I thought this was supposed to be less stressful. Yet now, I am even more stressed. Now, I have a never-ending list *and* a sleigh that won't run. And oh, look at the time." Beatrix pointed at the invisible watch on her wrist. "Two days left until Christmas Eve. Three days until I break Christmas."

Megi scoffed. "You are not going to break Christmas. You know what you need to do." She pushed the phone in her direction, the number already up and ready to dial. Just one little push of a button and all her problems would be solved.

Beatrix snorted. "How about hell no." She pushed the phone back to Megi.

"Okay, girl, that's it." Megi stood and slapped her hands onto the table, rattling the hot cocoa. "I am tired, and I am going to bed. Do what you want, but remember, this is more than just you and some guy trouble. Get your shit together or else you will disappoint more than just a few million kids worldwide in the coming days. You'll disappoint everyone here at the North Pole, you will disappoint me, and you will disappoint your family. Now *goodnight.*"

Megi added emphasis to her goodnight and Beatrix stared at her in shock, mouth slightly agape. Never had Megi spoken to her in such a way. Beatrix nodded slightly and murmured, "Goodnight."

She watched Megi leave, and Beatrix wondered if she was being overly dramatic. Maybe...

She glanced at the phone and the number all queued up, ready to go. She took a deep breath to steady her temper and glanced out the glass walls of her small office. Below was the factory floor, and she watched the elves hard at work, as they had been for the last six months. Nonstop, 24/7 working in 12-hour shifts. As was always done at the North Pole, six months of grueling work, followed by six months of fun and relaxation. She didn't want the last six months to be all in vain.

With a sigh, Beatrix picked up the phone and hit the call button. The screen popped up, and with it, her face once more filled the small rectangle. She couldn't help but see she was even more bedraggled looking than earlier. Quickly, she grabbed the tie from her bun and loosened her hair, letting it fall past her shoulders, and shook it out. It wasn't the best, but it would do. What Beatrix couldn't hide, though, was the grimace upon her lips when *he* finally answered.

"Little Trix, I was wondering when you would call me." His voice felt slimy against her skin even through the phone, and Beatrix wondered how her father ever lasted doing business with the Krampus family. But this wasn't Krampus she was speaking to. No, this was his vile son. Unfortunately, they had the same name, so she had taken to calling him Junior. Which he absolutely despised. Junior flicked out his tongue and Beatrix swore she could feel him ogling her through the phone.

"Don't make this a bigger deal than it is, Junior. This isn't about you and me, it is about—"

"I'm going to stop you there, Trixi Babe." He held up a hand and smirked. "This isn't between your dad and mine anymore. You took over the business, as did I. And you know what I want in return for the magic to fix your sleigh."

"You vile, disgusting cocksucker. I will never—"

"You know what? I've changed my mind. Instead of you on your knees sucking my cock, I would rather it buried inside that sweet little—"

Beatrix ended the call with a choking snarl and hurled the phone across her office. It hit the glass door and exploded, black pieces of the phone intermixing with the clear glass door shards. She stomped across the office and grabbed the handle to the door, ripping it open. The rest of the glass broke, clattering to the ground.

The factory below went silent and Beatrix's face warmed as she took in all the elves' faces looking up at her. She turned on her heel and headed to the factory door. Grabbing her thick winter coat, she stepped outside and into the cold winter that was her home. She needed to clear her head and think about how she was going to save Christmas without sacrificing her dignity or calling for her father's help.

Chapter Three

BEATRIX TRUDGED THROUGH THE snow, muttering to herself. The day was brisk, and the sky was a clear, vibrant blue with no clouds in sight. A light breeze tickled at her face and Beatrix clenched her hands into fists. She kicked at a clump of hardened snow and watched it go flying over the embankment in front of her. Then she kicked another clump for good measure, imagining it had Junior's face on it. This one sailed right over the embankment to hit something with a dull thud.

A growl reverberated through the forest Beatrix stood in, and only then did she realize how far she had wandered. She was near the old wishing lake, a place she had not been since she was a child. Beatrix ran up the embankment and paused at the top, taking in the growling entity below. A man, tall and athletic, with broad shoulders and chiseled abs, stood at the lake's edge. A large set of six pronged antlers blossomed from his head and as Beatrix's eyes took in his entire form, a blush heated her cheeks. He was completely naked. The man lifted his gaze, a snarl on his lips as he spotted her. "Why are you throwing snowballs at me?"

Beatrix blinked rather stupidly until her brain finally caught up with his words. Then she scowled. "I wasn't throwing snowballs. I was kicking them, and it wasn't at you. You just happened to be in the way."

The man scoffed and turned away, giving Beatrix a half-hearted wave, as if to tell her to move along. Frustration constructed over the last few months finally spilled forth and she slid down the hill, more than ready to give this man dressed in reindeer antlers a piece of her mind. Yet as she came closer, and he turned toward her once more, Beatrix was able to see him clearly. The antlers were no costume, and his ears were longer then normal, flicking in annoyance like that of a reindeer. In fact, she ogled the naked man in front of her, not because he was naked but because she swore his tanned skin wasn't actually tan, but a soft layer of fur.

She reached out, entranced, and not thinking. The man snorted, visibly radiating with annoyance, and grasped her wrist before she could make contact. His hand was calloused and warm.

Fingertips and nails blacked, but not with frostbite. It looked natural. Beatrix tried to snatch her hand back, but instead the man yanked her forward, flush with his chest.

Snowflakes whirled around them, but when Beatrix looked at the sky, it was still clear. She frowned and met the man's gaze. His eyes were dark, so dark she swore they were black, and he tipped his head, careful not to hit her with his antlers, which she could see now were not a prop. His hair was almost as wild as hers and it draped over her as he nuzzled her neck and breathed in deeply.

Beatrix held her breath, too afraid to move in case she accidentally skewered herself on his antlers. She felt the rumble in his chest, his hot breath against her neck, and she wasn't sure what to expect when he pulled away from her. His eyebrows furrowed, mouth thinning.

The seconds ticked by, snow flurrying around them, and when he finally spoke, it was low and angry. "Why did you summon me, Daughter of Claus?"

Beatrix shook her head. "I didn't summon anyone. I... oh—" She stopped mid-sentence. The man standing before her *was* covered in a layer of fur like that of a reindeer in the summer, hands blacked as if they should be hooves, and he had the most impressive set of antlers she had ever seen. Her mind went back to earlier in the day, and Beatrix stared at the man in disbelief. "You can't be him," she whispered.

The man leaned down, face coming to within an inch of her own. His hot breath tickled across her face. "Can't be whom?"

"The Reindeer King," she breathed out and the man in front of her smiled.

"That I am, little Claus."

A biting chill kicked up around them, entrapping Beatrix and the Reindeer King in a vortex of snow. He reached out, grabbing Beatrix by her upper arms, and without a moment of hesitation, his mouth was on hers. A startled harrumph echoed from Beatrix, and she pushed away with all her strength.

"How dare you!" Her voice echoed, and the Reindeer King let her go, taking a step back with a twisted smile. Beatrix had her fist raised, ready to punch the Reindeer King, who had stolen a kiss from her, until she looked around. Her jaw dropped.

Gone were the snow drifts and lake. Instead, Beatrix found herself surrounded by slate gray rock walls and flickering torches. She spun in a circle. There was no exit that she could see. Only a lone throne, covered in animal pelts sitting in the middle of a cold cave. The Reindeer King stalked away and sat on the throne, his twisted smile dropping to a frown.

"Are you not happy?"

Beatrix stared at him, dumbfounded. "You just fucking kidnapped me!"

The Reindeer King frowned even harder. "You are not a child."

"Abducted, relocated, stole... choose a word. They all mean the same thing."

"Ohhhhh, Reindeer Kinggggg! Reindeer King, I am waiting for youuuuu. Come and steal me away," he sang, mimicking Beatrix's voice the best he could.

Beatrix stared at him, slack-jawed, before her eyes drifted down his body of their own accord. She snapped them back up to the Reindeer King's face and snarled, "One, that was a joke. I did not summon you, nor did I give you permission to abduct me. Secondly, put on some fucking pants. I can't concentrate with your dick hanging out."

Silence hung in the air as they both stared at each other, Beatrix trying her hardest not to let her gaze wander once more. The Reindeer King cocked his head. "You do not want to rut with me?"

"Absolutely not!" Beatrix's shrill words bounced off the cold cave walls. She turned away from the Reindeer King and ran up to one of the walls, her hands sliding over the smooth stone. She needed to find a way out of here. She didn't have time to argue with an obviously delusional Reindeer King.

"Lies." The deep voice came from right behind her and Beatrix spun, palms outstretched, ready to push him away from her. Her hands landed, but he didn't move an inch. Beatrix's breathing deepened, heat creeping up her face as she left her palms flush with his warm furred chest.

"I'm not... fine. I find you insanely attractive, but I don't have time for this," she whispered.

He leaned in, pushing her against the stone wall. "In this place, all we have is time."

Beatrix glanced into the Reindeer King's dark eyes, one of her hands sliding from his chest to tangle her fingers into his wild and long, dark brown hair. "What do you mean?"

The Reindeer King leaned in even closer, his lips almost touching hers. "This place lives between the veil of time. A day here is but a second in yours. Here you have all the time you could ever ask for."

Beatrix's breath hitched as the Reindeer King closed the distance between their lips and stole another kiss from her.

But this time, she didn't fight him.

Chapter Four

Beatrix sank into the kiss as the Reindeer King claimed her mouth, his tongue tangling with hers. She moaned, arching her back as his hands grabbed her ass. Beatrix wasted no time, unzipping her jacket and pulling at the red coveralls she was still wearing from earlier today. They fell to her knees, only to tangle around her ankles and boots.

The Reindeer King broke the kiss and swung Beatrix into his arms, making his way over to the throne. She took the opportunity to kick off her boots and the tangled coveralls. He rumbled low in his chest as he sat, placing Beatrix on his lap, facing her away from him. His hands gripped her thighs, spreading her legs wide, wide enough to hang off the arms of the throne. The angle pushed her forward, and she leaned down, hands sliding over his powerful thighs. His fingers dance over the lace of her panties and Beatrix gasped as the sound of fabric tearing echoed through the cave.

She pushed back the tangle of her hair and looked over her shoulder, ready to give him a piece of her mind for tearing her favorite red underwear, but the words stuck in her throat. The Reindeer King had a look on his face, like that of a man who was dying of thirst, and she was his only water source. He massaged her ass cheeks, eyes hooding slightly before he caught Beatrix looking at him. His lips twitched into a sinister smile, and he slapped her already throbbing pussy. Beatrix gasped and bit back her moan as he sunk a finger into her wet folds.

"Already so wet for me," he murmured and withdrew his finger, slapping at her pussy again. This time he sank in two fingers and Beatrix's moan ricocheted throughout the stone cave. "That's a good little Claus. Moan for me."

Beatrix arched her back as the Reindeer King continued to play with her, sinking in a finger or two only to pull out almost immediately to slap her soaking wet pussy. Her hands gripped at his shins relentlessly, nails digging into flesh and soft fur. She was on the edge of spasming around two of his fingers as he sank them into her again, but this time when he pulled back out, he ran a hand up her spine to grab the back of her neck. His hand twined into her hair, gripping her scalp, and Beatrix felt the tip of his cock press at her entrance. She held her breath, waiting for his thick head and shaft to fill her, her pussy already tightening in anticipation. He pushed in an inch before pulling back out and let his cock slap against her entrance.

Beatrix cried out, begging as he pushed in again, only an inch deep before pulling out. "Please, please, I need more."

The Reindeer King chuckled, massaging her ass with his free hand before a snap echoed through the cavern. A bed of furs appeared out of thin air in front of Beatrix's face, and she gasped in surprise as the Reindeer King released his hold on her. He pushed her off the throne and into the thick furs, aligning himself once more at her slick entrance before thrusting into her.

Beatrix cried out, her eyes rolling back as he continued to fill her. Her pussy clenched at the Reindeers King's thick cock, not wanting to let go as he pulled back, only to thrust deeply into her again. Beatrix came harder than ever before, the scream of pleasure ripping from her throat and echoing through the cave.

"That's my little Claus," he rumbled as Beatrix's pussy clenched tight around his cock again. Her hands gripped the furs tightly as he continued to pound into her from behind. His thrusts became erratic and seconds later, the Reindeer King bellowed and Beatrix felt him pulse inside of her, filling her up as he came. His weight pressed against her back, sinking Beatrix into the warm furs. She sighed, letting the afterglow of her orgasm seep into her overburdened mind. The Reindeer King pushed her hair out of the way to stroke her neck. "You have soot on your luscious skin, little Claus."

Beatrix groaned and shoved her face into the furs. And just like that, the afterglow was gone, the reason for why she had grease all over her coming rushing back to the forefront of her mind. "It's not soot. It's grease."

Another snap echoed through the cave and with it came the sound of rushing water and delicious steam. Beatrix lifted her head, and her eyes widened. Where there was once a plain stone wall now stood a small in-ground pool, equipped with a cascading waterfall. Lush green moss with white star-shaped flowers decorated the back wall and surrounding area around the steaming pool.

The Reindeer King planted a soft kiss against Beatrix's neck before sliding out of her. She bit back her protesting moan, only to gasp as he reached down to scoop her up into his strong arms. He led her over to the pool and placed her down on top of the soft moss. Beatrix dipped her toes into the warm water and closed her eyes, bliss surrounding her mind.

Quickly, she unclasped the bra she was still wearing and tossed it to the side before sliding fully into the pool. It took her a moment to realize the Reindeer King had not followed her, instead sitting at the base of the water. She turned to face him, and his gaze dropped to her tits. "Come here, little Claus."

Beatrix narrowed her eyes at the command and covered her nipples with her hands. "Make me."

A strangled sound, somewhere between a moan and rumble, reverberated out of him. His hooded gaze slowly rose, until their eyes locked. "Say that again and see what happens."

Beatrix gulped, her heart starting to beat rapidly. His gaze was intense, his tone as if he was baiting her, challenging Beatrix to make him come and get her. She took a step back, accepting his unspoken challenge, and grinned. "Make me."

Chapter Five

THE WATER ROLLED, SPLASHING Beatrix as the Reindeer King slowly stalked toward her. She dashed to the left, trying to duck under his lunge, but he was too fast. He gripped the back of her neck, using her momentum to steer her body back to his. His free hand cupped her ass, pushing Beatrix back toward the rim of the pool.

Her breathing came out shallow as the Reindeer King's other hand came down to grip her other ass cheek. Her hands gripped his shoulders as he lifted Beatrix out of the water and placed her on to the soft moss. He nudged her legs apart, and she felt his cock harden once more. "Impressive," she murmured, and the Reindeer King chuckled.

"I know, little Claus."

Beatrix bit her lip as he cupped her boobs in his hands, massaging them before dipping down to kiss her. He broke the kiss to nibble down her throat before pushing against Beatrix's chest. She followed his silent command to lie down as he kissed and nipped his way down to her body.

By the time he reached her inner thighs, Beatrix had already wrapped her hands around the base of his antlers, body arching into his every touch. A sigh of satisfaction reverberated through the cave as the Reindeer King's tongue darted out to find her pussy. Beatrix rolled her hips up to meet the Reindeer King's face and tightened her grip on his antlers. She felt him smile slyly against her entrance right before plunging his tongue inside of her.

Beatrix cried out in ecstasy as the Reindeer King licked and sucked at her pussy. His tongue plunged in and out, swirling up to flick at her clit every so often. She didn't last long, her climax washing down her spine as she clenched around his tongue, still inside of her.

"Oh god!" she screamed as his tongue flicked out of her, his mouth covering her overly sensitized clit. He sucked and flicked the tip of his tongue as Beatrix squirmed, her pleasure almost on the brink of agony.

He finally slowed his torture to crawl his way back up Beatrix's body, and she wrapped her legs around his waist. He trapped her hands above her head, sucking at her neck before whispering into her ear.

"Next time you come, you will scream my name, little Claus."

Beatrix groaned as he teased her wet folds with his thick cock. "What's... what's your name?" she panted as the Reindeer King teased her with his cock.

"King," he murmured as he finally thrust into her. Beatrix cried out and arched her back, already constricting around him. He pulled halfway out and slammed into her again. His hand wrapped around her exposed neck, collaring her gently.

Beatrix was on the verge of another orgasm already, as she tried to stammer out his name. "Kin... Ki... King, I'm—" She couldn't finish her sentence before her pussy clenched so tight around King's cock, she wasn't sure how he was still moving inside of her. He dipped his head, swallowing her cry of pleasure, and Beatrix felt his thrusts becoming choppy. Twisting a hand free from his grip on her wrist, she thrust her hand into his tangled hair. She pulled none too gently, breaking his deep kiss, and he rumbled at her, eyes hazy with lust. "My name is Beatrix," she murmured against his lips.

King rumbled her name against her lips before tightening his hand around her throat. "Beatrix," he rumbled again with each thrust into her. He switched the grip on her wrist, tangling his fingers with hers. He claimed her lips again, and this time she swallowed his groan of ecstasy. When he pulsated inside of her seconds later, Beatrix smiled.

"Thank you," she murmured.

King glanced at her, confusion clear through his lust hazed eyes. "Thank you for what, little Claus?"

She took a deep breath before glancing away. "For taking my mind off of ruining Christmas."

King laughed softly against her neck. Beatrix scowled and tried pushing him off her, but he was too heavy. "This isn't funny. Why are you laughing?"

King pushed away slightly and had the audacity to tap her nose with his fingertip. "Don't be so serious, little Claus. All you must do is ask."

Beatrix narrowed her eyes and tried to flick his nose. He caught her hand and kissed her fingertips with a smile. "Ask what?"

"You know what?"

"Ask you to help me? Should I sing it just like how I apparently summoned you?"

Something flashed behind King's eyes, and he settled his weight back onto Beatrix. "Yes, yes, you should."

She eyed him suspiciously, but caved after a moment. "Okay." She took a deep breath and opened her mouth to beg the Reindeer King to help her save Christmas, but he took advantage of her open mouth to kiss her. When he finally broke the kiss, Beatrix pouted. "How am I—"

King interrupted her. "Yes, yes, I will help you. On one condition."

"Fine, what is the condition?"

"I want to come with you," he murmured softly.

"Come with me where?" Beatrix asked, slightly confused.

"To help spread the Christmas cheer. It's something I've always wished for."

Beatrix softened underneath him and nuzzled her nose into his neck. "Well, I guess it's good you know a Santa who can grant you your Christmas wish."

King smiled and nuzzled Beatrix right back. "Let's go save Christmas then, little Claus.

Beatrix laughed and pulled King in for another kiss, echoing his words with a happy sigh. "Let's go save Christmas."

The End

Valentine's Arrow

Holidays After Dark

Astrid Vail

Blurb & Content Warning

After losing her job and relationship in one fell swoop, Arrow stumbles across a listing requesting help to plan a Valentine's Day bash.
Only there is one problem.
The address listed is in the Night City, a place full of demons, shifters, and everything in between. A place no respectable fairy such as herself should wander into.
But the Night City is not what it seems and one little mishap later, Arrow finds herself face to face with the most gorgeous man she has ever seen.
Now Arrow can't help but wonder...
Could the Night City and the man she finds herself instantly enamored with be the new beginning she needs?

Valentine's Arrow is a short M/F paranormal erotica that includes graphic sex scenes and adult language.

Chapter One

"WHAT DO YOU MEAN, terminated?" Arrow yelled, her voice hitting a shrill pitch.

The Grand Mistress of Fairies Grace looked down her nose at Arrow. "This institute does not tolerate lawless behavior in any manner. We do not employ anyone with a record."

Arrow's mouth dropped wide. "You, you, you have got to be kidding me! All I did was glue his wings together. He was the one who—"

The Grand Mistress held up her hand. "Enough. You held a temp position to begin with. You can return to the job agency and find another job. Now get off the property."

Arrow snapped her mouth shut and floated back down to the ground. In her anger and disbelief, her iridescent wings had gone into hyper speed, pulling Arrow a few inches off the ground. She turned and stomped down the hallway, through the imposing open doors of the college, and launched herself off the stately steps into the sky.

The angry buzz of her wings kept the few other fairies flying around out of her path, and soon Arrow found herself in front of the temp agency. She landed in line and waited; the angry tap of her foot drowning out the surrounding whispers. The sun beat down on her head and shoulders relentlessly, and Arrow wished she had the foresight to have grabbed a light jacket.

And hat.

And sunglasses.

She sighed in defeat as the line moved up one person before immediately stopping. Arrow pushed at her short, dark brown hair. It was straightened into a stylish shoulder-length bob, but she sorely missed her long hair. Her hair naturally fell in curling locks, and she missed the way it used to bounce when it was up in a ponytail. Anger blossomed under her breastbone, and she glanced down at her hands. Nails, usually long and manicured, were now cut to the quick, pink nail polish chipping.

"Whatever," Arrow murmured. "He deserved a destroyed apartment. What's a few broken nails?"

The satyr in front of Arrow glanced over his shoulder before dismissing her words and going back to staring at the phone in his hand. Clearly,

Arrow was muttering to herself. They moved forward, another person in line, and she quickly lost herself in thought.

A few hours later, Arrow found herself seated in front of a pissed off looking elf. The elf sighed and slammed the file down on the desk. "No jobs will hire you until you do your community service."

Arrow threw her hands in the air. "It's not like I murdered anyone. *I* should be the one pressing charges. I mean, do you see what he did to my hair?" Arrow picked at the ends of her bob for emphasis, but the elf had no sympathy for her.

"Not my problem."

Arrow sulked in her chair and crossed her arms. "I'm not moving until you find me a job. There must be something."

The elf pursed his lips and shook his head before sliding a paper her way. "Here is a listing of community service opportunities. Come back once you complete your hours and we will see what is available."

She wanted to sulk longer, but the elf gave her a dismissing look before yelling out *next,* and Arrow slid off her chair in a daze. She wandered over to the massive doors, anger lifting her into the air. An older looking parchment caught her eye as she buzzed by the overflowing clipboard posting about upcoming events. She ripped it off the board quickly before buzzing away into the bright sunlit outdoors. A bench sitting empty on the perfectly manicured grass beckoned and Arrow landed on it. She uncrumpled the paper in her hand and read, hope slowly tumbling away.

Assistant Event Planner Wanted
Valentine's Day Bash
Come walk on the wild side and plan the party of a lifetime.
Call 876-4567

Arrow sighed. It was dated in the corner, for two years ago. Not only that, but the address in fine print listed the Dark City. A place she had only heard horror stories about. A place where certain beings roamed, and where the sun only shined a few hours a day. A city where night ruled supreme. All sorts of wickedness came from the Dark City.

Arrow worried at her bottom lip. She briefly wondered if the party ever happened. And why had they advertised for it here? In Fairy City, of all places.

The sound of a voice snapped Arrow back to reality, and she scowled. Across the grassy courtyard stood her ex and his gaggle of friends. A pretty fairy, scantily clad in a light green flowing gown, with long curly blonde hair clung to his arm. Arrow cursed silently and clutched at the ends of her short hair. She wouldn't have been in this mess in the first place if her ex and friends hadn't gotten drunk and set her hair on fire. Then he had the nerve to cheat on her because he didn't think she was pretty without her long hair. His cruel words had pushed Arrow over the edge. In retaliation, she glued the bastard's wings together and destroyed his small apartment.

She watched them saunter away, and Arrow's chest grew heavy, sadness smothering her rage. With a deep breath, she pulled out her phone and dialed the number on the paper. It rang twice before rolling over to a voice mail.

"Leave a message."

Arrow hung up quickly and shoved the paper into her purse. She was insane to have even called the number. And what if someone actually had picked up? The Dark City was no place for her. Arrow instead looked over the other piece of paper listing all the potential places for her to do community service.

With a disappointed sigh, she called the first number.

Chapter Two

ARROW HAD LOST HER little fairy mind. It was the only excuse she could come up with as she landed on the dark cobblestone sidewalk. She glanced at the time on her phone and worried at her bottom lip. Currently, she was supposed to be doing her first hours of community service, digging trenches out in the garden district. Instead, she was in the Dark City, in front of a closed building, with dusk rapidly encroaching.

To be fair, it was only ten a.m., but the Dark City only got four hours of sunshine a day. Arrow pulled at her form fitted pink halter top, making sure it was tucked into her black jean shorts. Her matching pink work boots thudded against the cobblestones as she approached the door and knocked. The door didn't budge when she tried to open it. She leaned into the window and cupped her hands. It looked barren. Arrow squinted when she saw a shadow move and knocked on the window.

She waited a moment before taking a step away with a sigh. It was just a trick of the eye. Turning on her heel, ready to take flight, Arrow hesitated as the sound of a deadbolt being thrown caught her attention. She turned back around with a smile plastered on her face as the door slammed open.

It caught her in the forehead, and she stumbled back in shock. Pain exploded through her head and neck, and she slowly lifted her fingers. They came away tinged with blood. Arrow's heart raced, breath coming out in short bursts as she tilted to the side, and everything went dark.

"Oh no, no, no, no, no... I killed a fairy... I killed a fairy." Incessant muttering brought Arrow back to consciousness slowly. The low growl and sin-laden voice of a man had her eyes open instantly.

"You didn't kill her, Desi. Stop worrying."

Arrow shot upright into a sitting position before grabbing her head. A dull throb radiated through her skull, her neck stiff. "Ouch," she whined, before getting a good look at the two people standing in front of her. They both had the same silvered gray complexion and dark starry eyes.

The woman gave Arrow a look of pure relief, her fidgeting hands pulling at her long, dark black hair. She was tall and lithe in stature and all but danced around the living room she was in. But it was the man who caught Arrow's attention the most. His dark black hair was cut short on the sides, though longer on the top in a style Arrow could only describe as dangerous yet fashionable. His face masculine and handsome. A small smile tugged at the corner of his full lips, and he settled back into the chair he was lounging in. Arrow realized she was staring, her mouth slightly ajar, and the man winked at her.

"See, Desi, she is fine. Aren't you, Princess?"

Arrow blinked rapidly and flinched back as the woman, Desi, rounded the couch quickly and snatched Arrow's hands in hers. "I'm so sorry. You were close to the door, and it sticks. I just kicked it open, and... and... and why were you even at the door?"

Arrow was still reeling from being called princess by the sinfully handsome man who looked like he emerged from the night sky itself. It took her a moment to catch up with what Desi was rambling about. Though apparently not fast enough. Desi's face fell into panic once again.

"Val," she whined. "I think I gave her brain damage. Why isn't she speaking?" Desi turned back to Arrow. "Why aren't you speaking? Can you speak?"

"I'm sure she can speak, Desi. Just let her process."

Val's voice slid down Arrow's spine like living smoke, rubbing at her in ways she never knew a voice could. She was equal parts scared and aroused. "I can speak," Arrow whispered. "Can I have some water?"

Desi flew off the couch, launching into the kitchen with a loud clatter. Arrow winced at the banging of cabinets, and Val frowned slightly, his luscious lips tilting to the side. Desi was back on the couch moments later, water sloshing over her hands as it spilled from the glass. She carefully took it from Desi and sipped. The water cooled her parched throat even though it did nothing for the heat rising in her cheeks. Val was still looking at her and just his presence alone was getting Arrow hot and bothered.

Before her brain short-circuited and she did something deliciously wicked to him, Arrow turned her attention back to Desi. Pulling the piece of paper from her pocket, she handed it over.

"I know it's two years too late, but Valentine's Day is right around the corner and I, ummm... I know it's silly, but..."

Arrow trailed off as Desi stared at the paper in her hand. "Oh," she breathed before glancing over her shoulder at Val. He titled his head and gave Desi a curt nod. She turned back to Arrow, a large smile encompassing her face. "Are you offering to help with event planning?"

Arrow gave Desi a hesitant smile. "If you need the help still, I would love to be of service."

Desi jumped off the couch with a holler and began running around the room. "Yes! This will be amazing. This year will be so magical with a real fairy here!"

She zipped across the room, hugging Val before rushing over to Arrow and pulling her into a tight squeeze. The hug only lasted a moment before Desi zipped away, disappearing into the hallway only to return with a large planner in her hands. She slammed it onto the couch before Val interrupted her excitement with a cough. "Before you get too preoccupied, Desi. Don't you have a shift at the bakery?"

Desi blinked rapidly before a sheepish look crossed over her face. "Shoot, I do. I guess..." She glanced over at Arrow. "I guess you could leave your number and I'll call you?"

Arrow reached out, patting Desi on the leg. "Of course."

Desi grinned and ran out of the living room. Her goodbye echoed out as a door slammed and Arrow blushed, realizing she was now completely alone with Val.

And he was staring at her.

Chapter Three

Val leaned forward and lifted a finger to stroke his bottom lip. Arrow clenched her thighs together and clamped down the low moan in her throat that threatened to escape. Val was too attractive to be real. When the door hit her in the head, she really must have suffered brain damage.

Arrow peeled her gaze away from the way Val was stroking his lip, mind lost in thought, and instead reached up to prod at her forehead. It was a little tender still, but nothing to be concerned about. She was a fast healer, all fairies were. Arrow glanced back at Val and her breath caught. Before his gaze had been glazed over in thought, but now it was focused, and he was staring at Arrow like she was prey. His eyes followed her hand as she slowly lowered it back down to her lap. Then they dipped lower, taking in her bare legs. A smirk touched the edges of his mouth when he got to her pink work boots. A strangled noise echoed through the room and his eyes darted back up to Arrow's face.

She desperately pretended the strangled noise did not just come from her and glanced everywhere but at Val. She caught sight of an oval mirror high on the wall and jumped to her feet, wings moving vigorously to bring her up to the mirror's height. Arrow gasped at the sight of her tangled hair. Not to mention, there were smudges on her shoulders and arms. She could only assume it was grime from the cobblestones. Quickly, Arrow began running her fingers through her hair to untangle the mess. "I can't believe I look so terrible. I must look like a—"

A low rumbling growl caught Arrow off guard, and she turned slowly, hands paused in her hair. Val was standing right behind her, and her wings missed a beat, pausing for a moment. His hands shot out immediately, an arm wrapping around her waist while his other hand grabbed her upper thigh. Within a mere breath, Arrow was pressed against Val's chest. She grabbed his broad shoulders on instinct and her eyes widened as the look of bliss passed over his face before snapping back to neutral.

"Are you okay, Princess? I didn't mean to startle you."

Arrow shook her head and licked her suddenly parched lips. Val's eyes dipped and this time Arrow felt *and* heard a rumble come from his chest. "Are you purring?" She whispered before sliding a hand to his chest.

The rumbled deepened and Val rasped, ignoring her question. "I should put you down before I do something stupid."

"Like?" Arrow's voice cracked, lips going slightly ajar in shock at her own boldness.

Val's eyes hooded, hand from her thigh releasing and making its way up her side. His fingers lingered along her collarbone, before cupping her jaw. Arrow wrapped her legs around Val's waist, barely able to lock her ankles. He was so big compared to her, and an involuntary moan slipped from her lips. Her moan elicited a groan from Val as he wrapped his large hand around the back of her neck and captured her lips with his own. The kiss scorched Arrow down to her core, the fabric of her entire being lighting up with flames of desire.

Val pulled away and Arrow fisted his shirt in her hands. She jerked him back in, lips colliding once more. She parted her lips as his tongue demanded entrance to her mouth. As the most intense kiss of her life ensued, Arrow tugged at Val's shirt. She heard the buttons littering the ground over the rumbling in his chest. He fisted her hair and broke the kiss, to Arrow's dismay. His breathing was heavy, and he looked as distraught as Arrow felt.

"Something stupid like that," Val murmured, and she felt heat rush to her face.

"Oh," Arrow murmured as she unlocked her legs and tried to push away. Embarrassment flooded her veins and Arrow ducked her head, hiding her face with her hair.

Val tightened his arm around her waist with a grunt. "Princess, that came out wrong." Arrow peeked at Val's face through her hair and worried at her lip, taking in the crease between his eyebrows. Val sucked in a deep breath before continuing, "An hour ago, my sister knocked you out with a door. I just want to make sure you are okay before making any moves on you." He chuckled and added, "I don't even know your name."

Relief flooded her veins, and she gave Val a bright smile before scrunching her nose and rubbing at her forehead. It was still tender, but overall, Arrow felt fine. A low groan encompassed the room, and she met Val's eyes.

"Fuck, Princess," he murmured, and Arrow felt his chest hitch, the purring taking on a deeper cadence. He reached up, stroking the bridge of her nose lightly. "You are unbelievably adorable."

Arrow warmed at his words and the look he was giving her. She grabbed his hand and lowered it to her mouth. Nipping at his fingertips, she glanced at Val through her eyelashes, the tips of her lips hitching at the sides, when he groaned. "I would feel better if you kissed me again. And my name is Arrow."

The hand she was holding slipped from hers as Val cupped the back of her neck, fingers lacing into her hair. He pulled her close, lips scrapping against hers. "Arrow," Val whispered, and she blushed at the seductive way he said her name before kissing her again.

Chapter Four

SHE SANK INTO THE kiss, barely registering Val moving until her knees brushed against the couch. Val released her waist and his fingers trailed lightly across the bare strip of her skin between the top of her shorts and the hem of her shirt. Arrow whimpered at the touch, rubbing her front against his chest. She released her hold on his shoulders and pulled at the laces holding her shirt on. She didn't care if they were going too fast or if she was temporarily insane for wanting to get down and dirty with this relative stranger.

All she could think about was how good his bare skin would feel against her own. Val seemed to have the same idea as he shrugged his shirt off and threw it to the floor, along with hers. "Princess," he murmured as he placed his hand back on her. The one on the back of her neck tightened slightly.

Arrow whimpered and rubbed against him. He pulled back and nipped at her bottom lip.

Arrow gasped as he continued nipping at her lips before trailing kisses across her jawline and down her neck. Her wings fluttered as she felt pleasure building deep inside of her, straining for release. Arrow sank her hands in Val's hair, trying to pull him away before she did something silly like orgasm from just a few kisses.

Val lifted his head with a sly look encompassing his face and licked her neck, making his way back up her jawline to nip at her ear. Arrow's eyes rolled and her back arched as Val's fingers trailed up her spine. He dragged a finger across the edge of her gossamer wings and Arrow came undone, her pussy clenching tightly. Her breathless scream was obscured by Val's soft chuckle, and he kissed her lightly on the lips.

She opened her eyes with a groan, about to ask Val why he stopped, but the words dried up on her tongue. A fine misting of pink dust coated the couch and Val's arms and chest. Arrow's cheeks warmed in embarrassment. Never had she orgasmed so hard that fairy dust exploded from her wings. And here it was, coating them both. She shook her head, about to apologize, when Val caressed her jaw and rumbled, "Does it change colors with every orgasm?"

Her jaw dropped and Arrow choked on her words, "I... uh... I don't, umm... I don't know."

Val kissed her through the stammering sentence and lifted her off his lap. He spun her around, placing her on the top of the couch. Arrow gripped his shoulders tightly for balance as his hands tugged at her shorts. He pulled them off along with her very soaked panties. She didn't see where he threw them, concentrating solely on the look Val was giving her. His grin was wicked, and her pussy clenched with his next words. "We will find out together, Princess."

Val threw her legs over his shoulders and dipped his head. His hands grabbed tight on Arrow's waist, so she didn't career backwards off the couch. Val licked at her inner thigh and blew softly. Arrow ran her hands through his hair as he nipped and licked at her legs. She harrumphed slightly at the sight of her pink work boots still on her feet. She wiggled, eliciting a groan from Val. "My boots are still on."

"I am aware, Princess. But they are just so damn cute, just like you. I don't want you to take them off."

Arrow rolled her eyes, about to protest that men like heels, not pink work boots, when Val growled and licked her pussy. Her hands jerked in his hair, back arching, and Arrow was pretty sure her eyes crossed. "Oh, sugar tits," she moaned as Val swirled his tongue along her clit before nipping at it gently.

"Sugar tits." He chuckled before giving her pussy another good lick. "That's adorable."

Arrow wanted to say something, anything to keep the banter going, but her breathing grew heavy as Val's tongue lavished her, slow and steady. She already felt the low pool of pleasure in her core growing, building like a dam ready to overflow. Her toes curled in her boots, wings vibrating so hard Arrow was worried they would break away and take flight on their own.

Soft meowing sounds filled the room, along with the heavy rumbling coming from Val's chest. Arrow barely registered the meowing sounds came from her as her hands tightened in Val's hair. The pool of pleasure in her core spilled over and Arrow cried out as she shuddered. Val gave her one last lick before allowing Arrow to melt like a puddle into his arms. She wrapped her shaking arms around his neck and rubbed her face against his bare chest. Fingers tickled over her back, running up and down her spine. "Gold," Val purred, and Arrow blinked a few times, still reeling from her orgasm high.

"Gold?" she whispered.

Val's hands swept from her back to her head and into her hair, massaging at her scalp. "Gold," he purred again. "It does change colors. It's gold this time."

Arrow lifted her head and blushed. A fine mist of gold dust mingled over the pink, coating the couch, Val's chest, and shoulders. She bit her lip and pushed up to straddle Val's enormous frame and immense erection straining against her. With a grumble, she grabbed at the zipper of his pants. "I can't believe these are still on."

Val chuckled underneath her and tucked his arms under his head. Arrow rolled her eyes as she unzipped him, and his cock sprang out into her hands. Her eyes grew wide at the length and width, and for a fleeting moment, Arrow wondered if the massive thing would fit inside of her. She ran her hands down the length of his cock, marveling at it. Val's rumbling purr deepened at her touch and Arrow bit her lip. "Will it even fit?" she murmured.

Val groaned, hips jerking slightly as she squeezed him. "Princess, I promise you, I will fit."

He pulled at Arrow's hands, placing them on his shoulders as he sat up. Arrow had no choice but to move with him, straddling his lap. She was still so deliciously wet, and Val pulled her closer, hands gripped tight on her hips. Arrow wiggled and rubbed his cock against her entrance and clit. Her pussy tightened in anticipation of taking something so large inside of her. Val caught her mouth with his before positioning her hips and pussy over the head of his cock.

Arrow whimpered at the pressure as he slowly breached her entrance. He slid in an inch before pulling out. "Fuck, Princess. You're so tight," he whispered against her lips. He moved a hand from her waist to rub at her clit and Arrow groaned. She grabbed the back of his neck as Val slid inside again, this time a few inches farther. She knew he was going agonizingly slow so she could accommodate his girth, but Arrow wanted him fully inside of her that instant.

As he pulled out and plunged back in slowly, Arrow felt Val loosen his other hand to grab her ass. Arrow took her freedom and slammed her hips down. She came, hard and fast, as his cock impaled her and cried out in absolute pleasure.

"Arrow!" Val roared, too little too late, cock twitching inside of her. He grabbed her hair, forehead aligning with hers, and growled, "You are a naughty fucking Princess. We were going slow for a reason."

She giggled against his lips, and he growled again, hand tightening in her hair. But instead of pulling back out, Val ground his hips in a circular motion, eliciting a small squeak of pleasure from Arrow. He continued his slow bump and grind, gripping Arrow in a way where she was trapped in his embrace. She held onto him, enjoying the ride.

Her eyes crossed, breathless moans and pleasure-ridden squeaks filling the room every time Val bottomed out inside of her. His grip tightened and Val groaned, head dropping into the crook of her neck as Arrow felt his cock pulsate inside of her. The after waves of desire rolled over Arrow, her pussy clenching against Val's cock as he slowly pulled out of her.

"Let's go to bed, Princess," he whispered in her ear and Arrow sighed as Val scooped her up. She snuggled into his chest and drifted off to sleep right there in his arms.

Chapter Five

A LOUD THUD PULLED Arrow from her sleep, and she yawned against the hard, purring pillow under her head. Arrow blinked rapidly, and the pillow shifted under her.

"That tickles, Princess," Val rumbled and Arrow giggled. A soft sigh escaped her lips as his hand trailed up her spine and started massaging her neck. She sank into a blissful state of being, listening to Val's soft purring and barely registering the sound of footsteps echoing through the purrs.

"Val! Did the cute little fairy leave her number? Or did you scare her away with your drooling? And what is up with all this damn glitter?" The voice grew louder, footsteps landing right outside the door.

Arrow snapped her eyes open as Val's hand on her neck tightened. She turned her head in time to see the doorknob turn and squeaked in alarm. The door swung open, and Desi froze mid-stride, mouth hanging open in shock. Val's chest started shaking, a snort escaping as Desi shifted her gaze. A glowing hue surrounded her, and a loud snap echoed. Arrow scrambled off the bed in alarm.

In Desi's place, a large, obsidian dark panther now stood. It was the size of a small horse, with eyes glowing silver. Five tails dipped and swirled with invisible wind, serrated tail tips cutting into the door frame. Steam erupted from its snout and a low rumble echoed through the room. Arrow was still staring in disbelief as the pillow sailed across the room hitting the pnather in its face.

"Get out of here, Desi," Val grumbled. The monster in Desi's place turned and sauntered away. One tail snapped out and pulled the door shut with a loud thud. Arrow was still staring at the door as Val pulled her back into his embrace. She could hear her frantic inhales and could only imagine how wide her eyes looked. She was half convinced they were about to pop out of her head like a cartoon.

"You... you're... you... y..." Arrow stammered, teeth chattering.

Val sighed and leaned his head against the bed frame. "Yes. We are Hell Cats."

Arrow sucked in a loud breath and instantly clamped her hands over her mouth. A scream built in the back of her throat, and she had to fight to keep it down. "But... but... I thought Hell Cats..." Arrow stammered.

Val remained quiet, letting the silence build until it became apparent Arrow wasn't going to finish her sentence. His chest rumbled, hand running up the length of Arrow's spine. "That we are all evil? And like to eat fairies?"

Arrow bit her lip and nodded slowly, still too scared to say anything.

Val snorted and shook his head. "A nasty rumor started over a century ago when our cities split. On the contrary, I particularly like fairies. And I really like the one sitting on my lap right now. Even though, in hindsight, I should have told you what I was from the start."

Arrow peeked a glance at Val's face. His eyes were still closed, head leaning back against the bed frame. "Were you scared I would run away if you did?" Arrow whispered, and Val smiled softly.

"I was more thinking along the lines of how lucky I was that the prettiest fairy in all the lands somehow landed on my couch."

Arrow tsked and smacked Val on the chest. "Oh, stop it."

Val rumbled and cracked an eye open. "Stop what, Princess? Stating facts?"

Arrow giggled as her panic melted away, and she turned in Val's arms. "So, you aren't going to turn me into fairy mince meat and gobble me up?"

Val shifted, hand running down Arrow's thigh. He pulled at her legs, and she ended up straddling him. "I never said that," he purred.

Arrow blushed as Val moved his way flat on the bed and pushed her farther up in the process. She gasped as his hot breath grazed her inner thighs and moved to grab the headboard. His hands massaged her ass as his tongue danced wickedly across her pussy. Arrow groaned in pleasure, and she closed her eyes. Her hands fell from the headboard, weaving through Val's silky hair as her hips took on a life of their own.

She rode Val's face as their groans of pleasure filled the silent room. Much too soon, Arrow felt the heat building within her explode outward as she came. A shiver slid down her spine as Val gave Arrow one last lick before letting her slide off his face. He scooped her limp body into his arms and tapped her nose gently. Arrow gave Val a lazy smile, "I stand corrected. Maybe I do want to be gobbled up by the big bad Hell Cat."

Val laughed. "Come now, Princess. Let's shower and maybe this big bad Hell Cat will make you something for breakfast."

Chapter Six

ARROW MUNCHED ON AN apple slice as Val rolled his eyes, listening to the other person ramble over the phone.

"Fine, I'll be there in twenty minutes." He hung up with a curse and glanced at Arrow. She fought a blush as her entire body simmered from his gaze. He reached out, ruffling her semi dry hair. "Princess, I have to go to work. Promise not to run away while I'm gone?"

Arrow smiled. "And what would happen if I ran away?"

Val purred, eyes hooding as he leaned into her space, his lips scrapping against hers. "I would just have to chase after you."

Arrow lost the fight and felt her face turn red at the thought, her breathing already going shallow. She groaned in displeasure as Val leaned away and straightened his tie. Arrow had to admit, he looked spectacular in a suit. It did nothing to mask his gorgeous frame. Quite the opposite. It emphasized every delicious part of him.

He blew her a kiss before stalking out the door and Arrow sighed. She spun the chair she was in and almost fell off in fright as she came face to face with Desi, back in human form. Her hand flew to her chest, heart beating a mile a minute. "Desi, you startled me."

Desi smiled and pushed the party planner book in Arrow's direction. "Now you are mine for the day," she purred with absolute glee.

Arrow narrowed her eyes, but didn't say anything as she pulled the planner closer and started thumbing through it. About twenty minutes later, Arrow slammed the planner shut and glared at Desi. "Why are you staring at me like that?"

Desi grinned widely, showing off her pearly white teeth. She propped her chin on her hand and a dreamy look overtook her face. "I'm just happy."

Arrow rolled her eyes. "Let's just concentrate on the event you want me to help plan. You have some good ideas in here, but I need to know more about the city and what will attract people to sign up on such short notice."

Desi snapped to attention, giving Arrow a mock salute, "Yes, ma'am. Well... first, a real-life fairy will attract attention. So that's a plus."

Arrow frowned and shook her head. "I am so in the dark about this city. No pun intended. But if the citizens here want to see a real-life fairy, they could just take a trip to Fairy City."

Desi frowned and shook her head. "There are still a lot of misconceptions about the people and creatures here in the Night City. Most people don't go to your city because we don't want to cause a scene or scare you all."

"Oh... I, I guess you are correct. I mean..." Arrow blushed. "I had the same misconception. But I am beginning to see I was wrong."

Desi snorted and shook her head. "Oh! That reminds me. I forgot to ask. What even made you come out all this way?"

Arrow blushed and glanced away. She placed her hands in her lap gently, "Well... I got into a little trouble with the law and got fired because of it."

"What for?" Desi whispered and leaned in close as if Arrow were hiding a secret.

Arrow shook her head. "It was just something stupid. My ex and his friends were involved. It was an accident and my hair kind of caught on fire. But you know that wasn't what pushed me over the edge. He cheated on me. Because I wasn't pretty without long hair and I kind of lost it. I trashed his apartment, and he threatened to report me. Then all I remember is absolute anger raging through me. Next thing I know, my ex's wings are glued together, and I was arrested." Arrow finally took a breath and glanced at Desi. Her eyes had turned cold, silver fire flickering within. "Uhhhh..." Arrow faltered as a bit of steam snuck out of Desi's nose.

"I'll kill them. Just point me in their direction, and I'll—"

Arrow reached over quickly and squeezed Desi's hand. "I already took care of it. Hence getting fired and not being able to find a job in Fairy City. But it's fine. This incident wouldn't have pushed me to take a chance in coming here. And I wouldn't have met you or Val."

Desi smiled and Arrow opened the planner once more. She stared at the pages without really reading them, an awkward silence building. She started slightly as Desi reached over and placed her hand over Arrow's.

"My brother really likes you," she whispered.

Arrow sighed. "Is it weird that I really like him too? But I can't explain why I'm so instantly infatuated with him. I just am."

Desi snorted and shook her head. "No, it isn't weird. It's actually quite normal. We are all a bunch of shifters and predators in this city. We see what we want and chase after it. Insta lust is sort of part of the territory. And most of the time, it is because you found your mate. Chalk it up to animal instinct."

Arrow bit her lip, mulling over Desi's words. She pushed a stray lock of hair behind her ear, heart going a mile a minute. "Do... do... you think..." Arrow couldn't finish her sentence and Desi shrugged.

"What I think doesn't matter, but I've never seen my brother act this way before. Usually, he is much more reserved and intimidating." Desi sat straight up and frowned, trying to imitate Val.

Arrow giggled and shook her head. "Enough nonsense and talk about your brother."

"Who is your lover," Desi quipped and Arrow snorted.

"As I was saying, enough nonsense. I think I have an idea about the event."

Arrow's comment perked Desi up, shifting her focus, and she leaned forward. Arrow turned the planner around and pointed at two very different ideas.

"I think I know a way to combine these ideas seamlessly into one event."

Desi's eyes lit up and an impish smile overtook her face. "Now that... that sounds like a perfect idea."

Arrow smiled back. "Then let's get started."

Chapter Seven

ARROW BUZZED ABOUT, FLITTING across the grassy overlook and between a gaggle of people. She greeted them and sprinkled sparkling fairy dust into the sky, eliciting happy claps and smiles.

Vampires, demons, and shifters of all kinds arrived in batches; the event already sold out. Arrow buzzed into the red and gold dropped tent, snatching more vials of the fairy dust, which was actually a mix of colored sugar and glitter. She was about to take flight again, but a large chest blocked her way and Arrow squealed, jumping into Val's arms.

"Princess," he purred and caught her mid leap. The kiss he gave Arrow scorched her down to her very toes. She was breathless when Val pulled away and he chuckled before putting her back on the ground. "Princess," he purred again, this time glancing around the tent and everything beyond. "This is an amazing idea."

Arrow beamed from the praise. "It was actually you and Desi that gave me the idea. With all your chasing talk. Speaking of which..."

A couple emerged from the forest beyond with wolfish grins and wrinkled clothes. Arrow floated over and sprinkled some dust on them with a giggle before flying back to Val. They watched as the couple disappeared into the tent. The sounds of laughter and glasses tinkling warmed Arrow's heart. Desi emerged a few minutes later and headed over to Arrow and Val. She was bouncing from excitement, the plastic clipboard in her hands slightly cracked. Arrow snorted and snatched it away from her. She flipped through the list of names and checkmarks. "That was the last couple, right?"

Desi spun around and glanced at the sky. "It was, and just in time, too. Arrow, you are a freaking genius. I can't believe you set up the moonlit forest chase and a sunrise banquet to coincide. You timed it perfectly."

Arrow blushed and shook her head. "I wasn't that hard. I just liked both the ideas."

Desi laughed and glanced at Val. "Wasn't hard, she says. I'm pretty sure she hasn't slept in two days." She looked at Arrow. "You also look super tense."

Val gave Arrow a sideways glance and a grin that melted her panties off. "Hmmm... I can think of something that might relax her a bit. Since she has been so busy for the last two days."

Desi jumped up and down, "Yes! You two should take part in the forest chase." She turned toward Arrow. "You will have so much fun. I promise."

Arrow bit her lip, glancing to the sky, which was already lightening, and then to the drop tent. "Are you sure you can handle the sunrise banquet by yourself?"

Desi tsked and snatched the clipboard away from Arrow. "Pleaseeeee, I can totally handle it. Now go. Have some fun."

Arrow blushed and glanced over at Val and the forest behind them. "So do I just..." She motioned a hand toward the forest.

Val winked at her and loosened his tie. He pulled it over his head and kicked off his shoes at the same time. Arrow's eyes widened as a low growl rumbled from his chest. "Run, Princess."

Arrow didn't need to be told twice as she sprinted away and took flight. She stayed low, zigging and zagging through the trees. Excitement and adrenaline flooded through her veins as Val chased after her. Time blurred, only the excitement of being pursued filled her thoughts. She was in the middle of zagging around a tree branch when a powerful hand wrapped around her ankle and yanked Arrow out of the air.

She squeaked in surprise before laughing as Val's muscular arms wrapped around her. He toppled them to the soft forest floor and suddenly his lips were on hers. Heavy breathing mingled with moans, hands tearing at clothing. Val turned her around, hands at her hips angling her butt up while Arrow lowered her arms and chest to the ground. Val growled as he trailed a finger up her already slick entrance.

Her pussy throbbed for his touch and clenched as he slowly thrusted a finger inside. Arrow moaned and sank onto the ground lower, legs widening. The soft forest floor was damp against her bare knees, soft and forgiving unlike Val's cock, which was already demanding entrance into her wet folds. "Are you ready for me, Princess?"

"Yes, yes, please," Arrow pleaded as Val worked himself inside of her. The angle was deep, and Arrow moaned, gripping the forest floor beneath her fingertips. Her eyes rolled back, pussy throbbing. Heat pooled steadily inside until it spilled over, pussy clenching and releasing against Val's cock as he bottomed out inside of her. Fingers trailed up her spine and Val grabbed her gently on the back of the neck. His fingers wove into her hair, his other hand coming to the ground next to hers.

He was careful not to squish her wings between their bodies as he rode her. His thrusts slow and deep as Arrow's moans filled the morning air.

Pleasure coiled through her again, making its way down her spine to the tips of her toes.

"Fuck, Princess. Keep moaning for me," Val rumbled as his cock got even harder inside of her.

Arrow felt him pick up speed and her orgasm spilled over once more as Val released inside of her. She collapsed to the forest floor, completely spent, her body riding a pleasure high.

Val bundled her in his arms and Arrow laid her head on his hard chest, listening to his rapid heartbeat intermingling with purring. Reaching over, Arrow interlaced her fingers with his. A smile blossomed on her face as Val lifted their clasped hand to his mouth and kissed her fingertips. "I missed you," he rumbled and Arrow giggled.

"I was only two days. Plus, you didn't even know me until four days ago."

Val nipped at her fingertips. "Doesn't matter, Princess. You're my favorite meal and I want it daily. I want to hear your moans of pleasure and feel you clenching around my cock like you can't get enough of me. Because I can't get enough of you."

Arrow pushed away from Val's chest and straddled him. She leaned down and gave him a kiss, licked at his lips and murmured. "I'm your mate, aren't I?"

"Yes. I knew it the second Desi brought you into the house. But we can take it slow, Princess. I don't want to rush you."

Arrow scoffed and shook her head. She gave Val another kiss. "I don't want slow. I want you."

Val chuckled and wrapped his arms around her. "Good. Because you have me. Happy Valentine's Day, Princess."

"Happy Valentine's Day, my mate," Arrow whispered back and snuggled into the warm embrace of Val's arms to watch the sun rise on the happiest day of her life.

The End

Fireworks In the Bayou

ASTRID VAIL

Blurb & Content Warning

Home is where the heart is... or in Reggie's case, home is where her mate is.
Reggie is ecstatic to finally head home after two years away on a research fellowship. All she wants is some good food, much needed pack time, and space for her inner wolf to run.
Except fate has something even more exciting planned for her return.
The last thing Reggie expected to see is the shy vampire waiting to pick her up and bring her home. But one sniff tells her something much more intriguing.
This vampire is her mate.
From awkward first impressions to a night under the firework lit sky, Reggie is determined to unleash her mate's wild side and show him what it means to be mated to a bayou shifter.

HOLIDAYS AFTER DARK

Fireworks in the Bayou is a sweet and spicy paranormal erotic short story centered around the Fourth of July.
Content warning include explicit sex scenes and crude language.

Chapter One

REGGIE

"Operation Home Bound is a go," Reggie squealed as the transmitter on her watch pinged. She had T-Minus six hours to get everything in her small dorm packed and ready to go. Then she would be heading home for good.

The wolf inside of her stirred and growled in her mind. *"Good, I don't like this planet. No good running spots."*

Reggie rolled her eyes and muttered, "There are perfectly good running spots. You're just being picky."

"They aren't home."

Reggie sighed. Now that was the understatement of the year. Or really, the last two years. She stepped over her half-packed travel bags and pulled back the curtain to the only window in her room.

Reggie's dorm was part of a bigger living complex set up to house the researchers, security, and everyone else living on this small planet she called home for the past couple of years. The lilac-colored sky was darkening, silver stars starting to shine as they made their nightly assent. The moon was absent tonight, and her wolf huffed in disgust.

"Oh, come on, you can admit it is gorgeous here," Reggie whispered as she took in the dark green rolling planes, with the spattering of shimmering gold and red flowers.

"Not home. Not the bayou. Hate lifeless lands," her wolf grumbled and flexed her large paws in her mind.

This time, Reggie scoffed. "Lifeless? This planet is teaming with life. Just last week you were chasing the sea birds down at the beach."

"Doesn't count. We need to go home. It's time."

"We still have six hours until our flight, and I need to pack."

"Leave it. It's just stuff. Let's go now."

Reggie snorted and shook her head. "No. We are not leaving everything behind. And we can't leave any earlier. Why are you in such a rush?"

"Just want to go home. Miss the pack. Family. And..."

Her wolf paused, and Reggie frowned. It wasn't like her wolf to hold back on speaking her mind. "And what?"

"I can feel it. The pull, the need. The ache in our bones. Our other half is calling."

Reggie dropped the shirt she had just picked up to put into her luggage. Her mouth went dry, mind spinning. "Are... are you saying what I think you are saying?"

Her wolf snorted and pawed at her mind. *"Yes, our mate awaits on Earth. At home, in the bayou. Let us go claim them."*

Reggie squealed in excitement, prancing across her room. Finding one's mate was a rite of passage among shifters. It didn't matter that she was twenty-six and had masters in Botany and Plant Pathology. It didn't matter that they picked her out of thousands of applicants to go into space and intern with a prestigious research team on a newly found planet. To a shifter, the rite of passage into adulthood was when you found your true mate. Your other half. Sure, the pack and her parents were proud of everything she had accomplished, but they would be beyond ecstatic to know she had also found her mate.

Well... almost found her mate. She just had to get back to Earth and Louisiana first... then sniff them out. But she trusted her wolf. And if she was telling Reggie their mate was there, then she believed her.

She glanced around her dorm room once more and got to work, throwing everything she could into her travel luggage. She couldn't wait to get home and chase down her mate.

"I swear I have the permit... somewhere..." Reggie mumbled as she stood at the unloading port back to Earth. She was digging around in her backpack, looking for the permit to get back home with her so-called contraband. They only labeled it contraband because she had yet to show her permit to the witch at the gate.

She smiled sheepishly at the male witch before her. He looked bored and slightly annoyed. Reggie's wolf growled in her head, pacing back and forth. *"Leave it. We will get more later. We are almost home. I want to feel the bayou under our paws. I want to drown myself in its scent and I want to find our mate."*

"I'm not leaving the fireworks. These are special and don't leave any chemical residue and ..." Reggie mumbled out loud before realizing it. She wasn't at the research facility anymore. She had gotten into the habit of speaking to her wolf out loud to combat the loneliness of not having other shifters around. But she didn't need to do that anymore. She ignored the stare the witch was giving her, suddenly interested now that she was talking to herself. "Sorry, my wolf was pestering me."

She got a 'humph' in response, and Reggie almost gave up searching for the permit, when her fingers felt something at the bottom of the pack. She pulled out the crumpled permit, allowing her the special fireworks produced on the merchant planet she had a layover on a few hours ago. They were special, just like she told her wolf, and not only did they not pollute the planet, but they also repopulated certain vegetation into the surrounding areas. She had put in the request a few weeks ago, when she found out the research grant was ending for the season. It also worked out perfectly that her homecoming would fall on the old American holiday of Fourth of July. She knew the pack loved any reason to celebrate and this would just add to the festivities of her finally coming back home.

Her cheeky grin spread across her face as she handed the permit to the grumpy gate witch. He scrutinized the permit within an inch of its life, but in the end waved her through. Reggie grabbed the fireworks package and stepped into the shimmering gate. She and her wolf sighed at the same time as the loudness of the Earth port greeted them, the smells of fast foods and coffee assaulting their nose. It was good to be finally home.

Another smell hit her, and Reggie almost tripped. It was a scent she had never smelled before, but she knew what that intoxicating and heady brew represented. Her mate was here. In the fucking

Louisiana Earth port, of all places. Her wolf had been right. Her mate was waiting for them here at home. So close to the bayou.

Her wolf in question rose to the forefront of their mind. *"Of course, I was right. Now let's find and claim them before they escape."*

Reggie turned in a frantic circle, sniffing like a madwoman, trying to lock down the scent again. It hit her, closer now, and she followed it to the left, toward the exit of the port. She scampered around the crowds, ran down the stairs and skidded to a halt in the middle of the large lobby and pick up center. She scanned the crowd and her eyes finally fell upon them.

Her mate.

And he was fucking gorgeous.

Reggie took in his dark blue eyes and shaggy, blonde hair. Her eyes roamed over his regal nose and strong jaw. She bit her lip as her gaze wandered farther down over his broad shoulders and lean body. He wasn't too tall, maybe only a few inches taller than Reggie herself, but she didn't care. He was her mate, and he was absolutely perfect.

Her eyes finally snagged on the sign he was holding, and she gasped in surprise. Her mate... he was here for her?

She wandered closer and drew in another deep breath, letting the scent of her mate wash over her senses. She was finally close enough to draw in other scents. He smelled clean and crisp, like a summer night out on the lake at home.

Reggie's wolf sighed in satisfaction before perking up. *"Oh, that's interesting."*

Reggie didn't say anything as she stopped a foot away from her mate, finally understanding what her wolf found interesting.

Holy fuck.

Her mate was a vampire.

Chapter Two

ISAIAH

ISAIAH DIDN'T WANT TO be here. He didn't want to be in Louisiana. He didn't want to be at this crowded Earth port. And he sure as hell didn't want to be waiting to pick up some random shifter and be her chauffeur for the day.

Yet here he was because his uncle wanted him to be here. *"It will be good for relationships between the vampires and shifter community,"* he had told Isaiah earlier this morning.

Isaiah grumbled under his breath, but his uncle was right. Tension between others in the supernatural community and vampires was something they dealt with for centuries, but times were changing, and they needed to start getting along. Shifter and witches outnumbered vampires five to one, and it wasn't like the vampires could go out and bite people to turn them. It was a silly and very old human myth built in complete falsehood. All supernatural's were born, not made. Including vampires.

Through Isaiah was more than ready to sink his teeth into something. He hated crowds. He just wanted to be at home, in an air-conditioned room, poring over old texts and learning about literally anything at this point.

He was so engrossed in his own sulking that he completely missed the cute woman practically flying her way through the crowd before she stumbled her way in front of him. His eyes widened; brows raised in concern as she gave him a sweet smile. His eyes roamed over her lush brown hair that fell over her shoulders in a wild wave. She was wearing a pair of well-loved and torn up jeans, black sandals, and a gray tank top with a dark green plaid button-up over it. Her body was full in all the right places, and his gaze finally made it back up to her face, with her cute button nose, and fuck... those bright hazel eyes. Isaiah was instantly jealous of whomever was picking this cutie up. She seemed so laid back and down to earth. The complete opposite of him. He swallowed painfully as his fangs extended ever so slightly, pricking the inside of his lip.

The cutie wandered closer, sniffing the air ever so slightly and zeroed in on the sign he was holding.

She smiled even wider before prancing over on light feet and stopping a foot away from him. Holy shit, was she giving him googly eyes?

There was no way she was his pick-up. He was expecting a spoiled wolf shifter, not... her.

Isaiah glanced over his shoulder quickly, and the cutie in front of him giggled.

"I'm Regina James. But everyone just calls me Reggie. I can't believe I found you."

Her voice came out as a breathless pant, as if she was the one fighting for air. His brain bypassed her strange comment like she was looking for him specifically. No, she was just looking for her pick-up.

Stay calm, Isaiah, he whispered to himself. *And whatever you do, don't maul the cute shifter in front of you.*

Just the thought of sinking his fangs into her sweet neck was almost too much, and a strangled noise escaped him. Reggie's face turned to one of concern and she reached out to touch him.

Isaiah took a quick step back, putting the sign with her name on it between the both of them. He couldn't chance her touching him. He knew without a doubt he would lose it, right there in the middle of the crowded port. And the last thing the vampire community needed was an incident of him sinking his fangs into an unwilling wolf shifter. His heart sank as Reggie's face fell, her smile turning to a frown. Sadness crept through her pretty hazel eyes and Isaiah wanted to stake himself for making her look like that.

"Sorry..." he mumbled and glanced down at his perfectly polished black dress shoes. "I don't like being touched."

Isaiah inwardly winced and wanted to slap himself in the face for looking and acting like an awkward idiot. And he had just lied. He actually liked physical affection, and he knew it would be absolutely bliss if this shifter in particular touched him.

Reggie cocked her head, as if listening to unspoken words before giving him a shy look. She tucked one of her wild locks behind her ear and smiled. "No worries. I shouldn't have tried to touch you. Are you ready to..." She trailed off and motioned toward the glass doors leading out of the port and into the brightly lit afternoon day.

Isaiah nodded and gulped. Fuck, he would follow this woman all the way to the farthest end of an unexplored galaxy if she asked. Reggie started toward the door as Isaiah stuffed the sign into the nearest recycle bin and hightailed it after her. She was already outside, waiting for him, and he stumbled as the afternoon light cascaded over her beautiful body. Before stepping out, Isaiah donned his sunglasses and Reggie smirked. He hesitantly smiled at her, aware that he still had his fangs out.

His primal instincts were still telling him to drag this little shifter all over him and bite her, taste her, fuck her. Mark her as his. And he really, really wanted to give in.

"You know," she said. "Every time I see a vampire standing in the light of day, I always chuckle."

"Yeah, and why's that?" Isaiah teased her slightly, motioning to the car park.

Reggie snorted and tossed her hair back with a hand. "It's just that growing up, vampires weren't prevalent in my life. And I actually thought ya'll were night creatures, allergic to the day. The first time I saw a vampire was in the morning, in a little café, when I was in university. I dropped my coffee and just stared. Totally creeped them out. And to make matters worse, they were in the same class as me that semester. I was always that 'weird wolf girl' from then on."

Reggie laughed, her eyes sparkling from the light and memories, and Isaiah moved closer as they walked. "Yeah, it doesn't help that some of the most famous of us were recluses in the beginning. One actually did have major light sensitivity. That was when the daylight misconception came about."

Reggie mulled over his words, a slight flush warming her cheeks. "That makes sense. Most myths always start with a grain of truth. Like shifters, for example. We aren't blood thirst—" Her eyes got wide, and she glanced at Isaiah. "Oh... that was a bad analogy."

He snorted at her shocked look and shook his head. "No offense taken."

She mumbled under her breath, so low even his sensitive hearing couldn't pick it up.

"What was that?" he asked and took a step toward her, the distance between them becoming almost unbearable.

Reggie shook her head and giggled. "Nothing. Nothing. As I was saying, grains of truth are always prevalent in myths. Shifters were thought of to be vicious, uncontrollable animals. But that was because of one tiny incident a long, long time ago."

Isaiah watched her face, the way her lips moved as she spoke, and the way her nose scrunched up slightly. He nodded, so focused on the woman in front of him, he didn't realize they had stopped right in the middle of the car park. A blaring honk ripped them both back to the present and a gold sheen filtered over Reggie's eyes as she jumped in surprise.

She grabbed his hand and pulled him to the side as the car went around them, the driver giving them a death stare. Reggie immediately let his hand drop and shivered. Isaiah wanted to scream bloody murder at himself for making her think he didn't like physical touch. Instead, he pointed at a small red electric convertible. "That's us."

Reggie nodded silently and rushed over to the car, tossing her backpack and the package she was carrying into the backseat. She jumped in without opening the door and stared at him expectantly.

Right, he was supposed to be driving her home. That was all. That was all this was. Nothing more.

Isaiah pushed all his wicked thoughts to the back of his mind and got into the driver's side. He pushed the bottom to start the car and put on the navigation. "Where to?"

Reggie gave him a strained smile and typed in the address before turning back into her seat and staring straight out the window.

Isaiah suppressed his sigh as the navigation started talking and he pulled out of the car park, heading toward the outskirts of New Orleans.

Chapter Three

REGGIE

"TOUCH HIM. LICK HIM. Mark him. Fuck him," Reggie's wolf growled in her mind for the umpteenth time. It was starting to be her own personal mantra, and she ground her teeth as her wolf battled to take over. Reggie knew her eyes had to be flickering like fucking headlights by now.

"Stop it," she hissed in her mind. *"Our mate doesn't like touch, nor is he a shifter. We have to break the news to him gently that he is ours now."*

Her wolf howled in response and scratched at her mind. *"Mark him. Make him ours before anyone else can. Scent him."*

"Stop it," Reggie growled.

Her eyes grew wide as Isaiah cleared his throat, and Reggie realized she just muttered out loud again.

"Did you need me to stop the car?"

His voice was like the caress of a cool breeze on a hot and humid day. Reggie's wolf instantly settled down, and she wanted to reach inside her own head and strangle her. The little she bitch was making her look fucking psycho.

Reggie cleared her throat. "No. No. I was just, you know... arguing with my wolf."

Isaiah made a low noise in the back of his throat and nodded his head slightly. "That concept has always fascinated me. The fact that shifters have another being inside of them. Completely different from oneself, who they can converse with, like two spirits within one body. You can never be lonely."

Reggie glanced at Isaiah, surprised at his words. Most people didn't understand shifters were, in fact, dual spirited, two entities intertwined as one. Yet her mate did. And that made him even more mouthwatering. She wanted to reach out and touch him, to brush his messy hair away from his eyes. To touch those lips with her own. To caress her hand down his chest...

Do it, her wolf whispered.

Reggie gritted her teeth and tucked her hands under her thighs. "Yeah it's cool until your wolf starts to irritate the living hell out of you. Then it's like having an annoying sibling or parent suck in your head twenty-four hours a day. You can never get away from them."

Isaiah chuckled and Reggie wanted to record his laugh so she could listen to it over and over again. God, she sounded like a creep. She needed to take a chill pill and think about anything else.

Luckily for her, they started driving through New Orleans and the sights and sounds of her home distracted her mind. She smiled as all her familiar haunts passed them by. The city was in its off season, but even then, it didn't mean it was sleeping. Quite the opposite. In fact, the city lived and breathed as the locals and visitors alike milled about.

Soon they passed through, and the smell of the city faded, to be replaced by something much more lovely. The breeze turned cool as they drove down a winding road, cypress trees draped in Spanish moss surrounding them on all sides. The navigation told them to turn, and Reggie sat straight up, excited to be almost home. Then it hit her. There was no way in hell this vehicle was going to make it down the miles of muddy and swampy roads.

Reggie's wolf laughed in her head. *"Good. Make him walk us home. Seduce our mate."*

She sighed and pointed to a large dirt extension on the side of the road the pack used for parking. "You can stop over here. The car isn't going to make it down the road once it turns to mud."

Isaiah quickly pulled over and shut the engine off. A silence built between them. The only sounds surrounding them were of the bayou. Reggie closed her eyes and listened. She smiled as the sounds of the birds and wind rustling through the large cypress trees overcame her. When she opened her eyes, Isaiah was staring at her. Right, he probably wanted the crazy wolf shifter to get out of his car so he can go back to work.

Her wolf howled inside of her, yelling at her to take him right here, in the car, on the side of the road. Reggie gulped and smiled. She pushed a strand of her wayward hair behind her ear. "I'm sure you—"

"I promised—"

They both started and interrupted each other.

"Go ahead," they both said at the same time.

Reggie giggled and shook her head. "No, you please. Go first."

Isaiah gulped and glanced everywhere but at her. "I promised my uncle I would get you home safely. So, if you are walking, I can come with you, unless you would prefer me not to?"

Reggie blinked, dumbfounded. "Wait... you're not a chauffeur? For a company?"

Isaiah laughed and shook his head. "No. My uncle is the head of our vampire clan trying to make a home here in New Orleans. And he is trying to get in good with your parents, who you know are head of the local shifter pack."

He trailed off as Reggie sat there staring at him. "That's perfect!" she yelled and jumped out of the car, unable to sit any longer. "I was gonna ask you to come to the festivities tonight."

"Festivities?"

A worried look overtook her mate's face as Reggie came around to his door and opened it. She all but hauled him out of the car with a huge smile. "Yeah, festivities. Shifters love to have any excuse to gather and eat and have some fun. And my homecoming aligns with an old Earth holiday. There will even be fireworks!"

She dropped his hands and reached inside the open backseat of the car, grabbing her backpack and the box of fireworks. She shook it slightly. "Big boom. Lots of sparkles."

Isaiah smiled and shook his head, his shaggy hair falling over his forehead to cover his eyes.

Reggie reached out without thinking, brushing the hair out of his eyes. Their gaze locked, and it felt like someone had punched all the air out of her. She couldn't breathe, couldn't think, couldn't move. Even her wolf fell silent in her head.

Isaiah cleared his throat awkwardly and reached toward her slowly. Holy shit, was he going to touch her?

Reggie's whole body felt electric as his fingers grazed her shoulder, sliding her bag off and taking it from her. "I can carry this."

His whisper broke the spell, and Reggie snatched her hand back, tucking it into the back pocket of her worn out jeans. She nodded silently and pointed down the dirt road leading them farther into the bayou. "It's just this way," she managed to get out before brushing past him and walking away at a brisk pace.

Chapter Four

ISAIAH

FUCK. FUCK. FUCK.

Isaiah groaned internally. Could he be any more awkward with this flawless shifter? They had a moment back there near the car and he had to go and ruin it by opening his big fat mouth.

Sink your fangs into her, and your cock. Mark her as yours.

The inner darkness all vampires had in them rose to the forefront of Isaiah's mind. He pushed it back, but he was struggling against his most primal instincts, and he didn't know why. Normally he had no problem handling himself and his darkness, but there was something about this shifter that had him on the edge of his seat. He would follow her anywhere if it meant spending one more day with her. His gaze trailed down her luscious body, hanging onto every curve. He spent a long time admiring her swaying ass as they walked in silence. Her provocative scent was surrounding him, and Isaiah was pretty sure he was drooling.

Fuck, what was happening to him? Normally, he was content with his studies. He didn't go out, he didn't go to parties, and he didn't trail after women, drooling like a damn fool. Fuck, he was twenty-four and still hadn't even been with a woman. Well... maybe he had a few wet dreams before and read a lot of erotica for research, but that wasn't the same. Though he wouldn't mind practicing the things he dreamed about and read about on this pretty shifter in front of him.

Isaiah stumbled slightly, his foot getting caught, and he looked down, realizing just now that he hadn't been paying attention to where he was walking. His entire foot was buried in the muddied road, and he cursed. Reggie quickly turned around; her face slapped with confusion until she realized he was stuck in a mud puddle. "Oh! Wait, don't pull your foot out yet or else the mud will get inside your shoe!"

But it was too late, and Isaiah was already standing there, like a flamingo, with one socked foot in the air. Reggie rushed over and they both stared at his now ruined designer shoe, filling rapidly with swamp water. She sighed and got to her knees, rescuing his shoe and handing it to him.

"Well, you might as well go barefoot like me." She beamed up at him, and Isaiah realized at some point while he was drooling over her body, Reggie had taken off her sandals.

Sink your fangs into that pretty neck of hers.
Isaiah gulped.

His darkness was riding him hard. Something about seeing this gorgeous woman kneeling in front of him. Her head was in the perfect position to take his cock in her mouth. He felt himself harden in his slacks and it was taking all his willpower not to run his hands through her hair and unzip himself.

Reggie cocked her head as they stared at each other, and Isaiah dropped his foot into the mud, not caring anymore. He barely felt the mud as he slowly reached out and lost the fight. His fingers threaded through her hair, and she leaned into it, her hazel eyes clouding over with a gold sheen. A rumble filtered through the air, and Isaiah didn't know if it was coming from her or him. "Reggie," he whispered as she placed her soft hands on his shins, running them up to his thighs. "I don't know what is happening, but I don't want it to stop."

She parted her mouth, and Isaiah had to physically hold back the moan rising in his chest as she licked her soft, inviting lips. His gaze hooked on her uneven pulse, jack hammering away, and the slope of her sun-kissed neck. A bead of sweat trickled down, and Isaiah followed it with his gaze as it trailed over her tits and disappeared into her tank top.

Her hands clutched at his thighs and her labored intake of breath drew his gaze back to her flushed face. She opened her mouth, and the most beautiful words came spilling forth. "You're my mate. That is what is happening. I should have told you sooner, but I was..."

She trailed off as Isaiah's knees buckled and her hands trailed up his waist to his shoulders. His hand was still threaded through her hair as he grabbed her throat with the other one and pulled her closer. Their lips lingered a hair's breadth away, and Isaiah tightened his grip as Reggie moaned. Her lips parted even more as he held her still, studying every contour and inch of her face.

Of course, of course, that was why he was feeling this way. He was fighting against nature, against his very soul. Shifters had the unique ability to know who their mate was with just a single glance, and he knew better than to question her. He leaned in and captured Reggie's soft lips with his own without hesitation and as they parted under his, everything he was feeling clicked into place.

He was meant to be here and there was no going back.

He thrust his tongue inside, exploring every inch of her silken mouth. Fuck, if it was actually possible, he would explore this woman down to the very molecules of her soul. She moaned and leaned into him as her hands gripped and pulled at his button down shirt.

Isaiah pulled back, licking and sucking at her lips. He was careful not to catch her with his fangs, which was becoming extremely difficult. He needed to sink something into this divine shifter, whether that was his fangs, cock, or tongue again.

He groaned against her lips as the sound of ripping clothes filled the air and her hands were suddenly on his chest.

"Sorry, I just needed—"

Reggie started, but Isaiah pressed his lips against hers again. He pulled her closer into his lap and didn't care that they were essentially still sitting in a fucking mud puddle. Somehow, he knew his pretty bayou wolf would love to get down and dirty in the middle of the muddy road.

Fuck, he would get down and dirty with her anywhere she asked. His only preference was her. She was his fucking kink, and just the thought of burying himself inside of her sweet pussy made him almost cream his pants.

Her hands roamed over his bare chest, trailing farther down, and he thrust his hips up. When her hands gripped his throbbing cock through his slacks, his inner darkness loved the soft gasp she made into his mouth. He wanted his mate to make more sounds, just for him. Isaiah finally released her neck, his hand roaming to the front of her pants and popping the button.

Reggie panted against his lips, her hand griping his erection so sweetly through his pants as he unzipped her jeans and pushed his hand inside. His fingers slid over her soft curls and clit. Her hips surged forward as he circled her wet entrance before dipping a finger inside of her pussy. They both groaned, and Isaiah pulled out enough to add another finger. Reggie released her grip slightly to unzip him. Her soft hand against his raging erecting without anything in between them almost had him spilling into her hand.

He barely fought back his own orgasm as she began riding his hand, his palm rubbing against her clit as she stroked his cock. She whimpered against his lips, her pussy tightening around his fingers. Isaiah grasped her hair tighter, pulling her back slightly. He removed his fingers and hand from inside her pants and Reggie growled.

Isaiah chuckled and rolled them out of the damn mud puddle they had been splashing around in. Their first orgasm together wasn't going to be from each other's hands. No, it was going to be him driving his throbbing cock inside of her warm and wet pussy. He needed to feel her silken walls pulsating around his cock. He lay on his back and Reggie's eyes lit up as he forced her jeans down to her thighs. She leaned over him and managed to shrug a single pant leg off before setting herself back on his lap. The head of his cock dragged against her soaked panties before she pulled them to the side.

His hips lifted from the ground as Reggie wrapped her hand around his cock and lined it up with her entrance. All the air left his lungs as she lowered herself down, her tight little pussy fighting against his thickness. She growled, low in her throat as he filled her up, one inch at a time, until he finally bottomed out inside of her. He shifted his hips, moving with her as Reggie started to ride him. Fingernails dragged down his chest, and she threw her head back as harsh whimpers escaped her throat. Her pussy pulsated around his cock moments later, and he took control, hands to her hips, as she screamed out. He came two thrusts later, buried deep inside of his perfect bayou princess, his mate, his shifter goddess.

She glanced down at him, eyes glazed over in lust, and the sweetest smile touched her lips. Leaning down, she peppered his face with soft kisses. He groaned as his cock slipped out of her and she rolled over to the side. Once he got his breathing under control, Isaiah reached over and pulled her closer. He nibbled on the arch of her ear, eliciting a cute giggle. She slapped him playfully on his bare chest before sitting up and arching her eyebrow at him.

Just as he opened his mouth to tell her to get ready for round two, the sound of a truck engine cut him off. Both their eyes widened in alarm, and they scrambled up, getting semi dressed just as a truck came around the bend and skidded to a halt.

Chapter Five

REGGIE

THE TRUCK SKIDDED TO a halt in front of them, mud flying everywhere. Reggie wanted to be pissed, to yell at the person for running this moment with her mate. Her sexy and gorgeous mate, who she had yet to mark.

But a familiar head peeked out through the rolled-down window and Reggie couldn't stay mad. A smile lit up her face as her younger brother smiled back at her. "What the hell, loser! Mom sent me out to track you down. You should have been back hours ago."

He narrowed his eyes, a golden gleam overtaking them as he glanced over at her, then at her mate. "Why are you all muddy? And who is this jackass?"

Reggie growled as Isaiah positioned his body in front of hers slightly. Her heart melted at the protective gesture, but she grabbed his shoulder and sighed. "Isaiah, meet Luke, my idiotic brother, who doesn't have any manners."

Isaiah's tight shoulders loosened slightly at her words, and he glanced back at her.

She continued with a growl, pointing at her brother. "And this jackass is my mate."

Her brother stared at her in shock, opening and closing his mouth like a fish out of water. Reggie didn't give him any time to recover before interlacing her hand with Isaiah's and headed toward the truck. She grabbed the forlorn and muddied box of fireworks on the way. Setting it gently in the back of the truck, she gave Isaiah a half smile. "Sorry, he is a loud jerk. I can kick his ass if you want."

"Hey!" Luke called out, finally getting his wits back.

Isaiah snorted and pushed his haphazard hair out of his face. "Maybe later."

Reggie laughed as her brother muttered under his breath. She climbed into the bed of the truck and Isaiah followed closely behind. The truck jerked forward as her brother hit the gas with a holler and whipped it around in a fast three-point turn. Mud and water splattered all around them as Reggie collided into Isaiah's arms. She threw her head back in a laugh at the panicked face her mate was currently exhibiting. He hugged her tighter as the ride got bumpier, the tires slipping and sliding all over the road. Reggie leaned back into his bare chest, planting her feet against the truck bed, trying to stabilize them from rolling about and flying out onto the road.

Ten minutes later, they skidded to a halt in front of her parents' bustling front yard. Dozens of shifters, Reggie's entire family and their pack, were milling around the large picnic table, set up buffet style, eating and drinking. Luke flew out of the truck after it lurched to a stop, screaming at the top of his lungs. "I found her and her mate!"

Reggie dragged her hand over her face. Holy fuck, she was going to wring her brother's scrawny little neck, and she hadn't even been home for twelve hours. She forced a smile onto her face and glanced over her shoulder at Isaiah. He squeezed her hard around the middle and she could feel his heart beating a mile a minute in his chest. She kissed him on the cheek and brushed a bit of mud off his face. "Don't worry," she whispered. "I will protect you against my insane family."

Somehow, Reggie convinced her family and pack to let them both shower and change before peppering her and Isaiah with a million questions. She was currently outside of the main house, leaning against the porch railing, waiting for her mate to emerge from the house. One of the pack members, who was close to Isaiah's build, was kind enough to give him a change of clothing he had in the back of his car. And Reggie was able to scrounge up an old pair of jean shorts and tank top for herself from the attic. Her stuff had yet to be delivered Earth side, and her backpack was lost down the road somewhere. She grinned as her mom bounced up the stairs, light on her feet, and grabbed Reggie in a strong hug.

"Reggie, darling. Light of my life and pain in my ass. Why didn't you tell me you had found your mate?"

Reggie squirmed in her grip. "Mommm, I just found him. Quite literally, he picked me up at the Earth port."

Her mom threw her head back and laughed. "So that's Michael's nephew... Honestly, I told him not to bother sending him. I told him my daughter wouldn't get into a stranger's vehicle, even if we sent him to pick her up. But he insisted. So, I sent you a message on your phone to play nice with the vampire. Which you never responded to."

Reggie snorted and smiled. "Yeah, well... I smelled him the moment I got Earth side and never even had a chance to check my phone. Sorry about that."

Her mom shook her slightly. "It's fine. All is forgiven this time around. When it comes to mates, all common sense leaves our mind."

Speaking of which, her wolf pushed at her mind as the intoxicating aroma of her mate drifted closer. She wiggled out of her mom's arms as Isaiah opened the screened door and stepped out onto the porch, looking like a sexy, wet dream. Both Reggie and her wolf groaned, taking in the sight of their handsome vampire. The jeans he had on were a little big, hanging off his hips. He was wearing an open flannel long-sleeve, leaving his sculpted chest and abs bare. Reggie ran up to him and quickly placed her hands on his chest, dragging her nails over his pecs. She was hungry for his lips on hers and he must have had the same thought as he wrapped his arms around her and lowered his head.

"I'll just leave you two alone. But don't make the family and pack wait too long," her mom's voice echoed out, which Reggie promptly ignored. She pushed Isaiah back into the house and into the small living room. As she peppered kisses down the side of his neck, a low rumble emanated from his chest. Distracted, they hit the back of the couch and tumbled over it. Reggie laughed as they bounced off the cushions and landed in a tangled heap on the floor.

"Don't we need to go out and spend time with your family," Isaiah groaned as Reggie trailed kisses down his chest. She scraped her teeth over his nipple, and he grabbed her by the hair.

She shook her head and looked up, catching his heated gaze. "They can wait. My wolf wants to mark you, and I want you inside of me again."

Isaiah groaned, a red sheen slightly taking over his pretty blue eyes. "I want to mark you, too. And I..."

He paused and shook his head, a pink blush warming his perfect cheekbones. Reggie licked her lips. "And what? Please tell me it's naughty."

Isaiah took a deep breath. "I want to chase you. I want to pin you down out there in the bayou and fuck you until you're screaming my name in pure bliss. Then I want to sink my fangs into you and make you come all over my cock."

Reggie's mouth dropped open in shock. Who knew her mate was so naughty under his shy exterior? She gulped; her pussy was already wet from his words. She nodded and glanced toward the door and the loud pack waiting for them outside. They were just going to have to wait some more.

She smiled and jumped up, giving Isaiah a wink. "Catch me if you can."

Chapter Six

ISAIAH

ISAIAH SMILED AS REGGIE leaped to her feet and shimmied out of her shorts, then ducked out of her tank top. His mouth watered instantly, taking in her tanned and juicy body she presented before him like his own personal buffet. She winked and growled, "catch me if you can," before the surrounding air shimmered and in the blink of an eye, a light brown and honeyed she-wolf stood in her place.

Isaiah jumped to his feet, fast on her tail, as the wolf bolted out of the house and veered to the left. She glanced over her shoulder to make sure he was still following her before disappearing into the thick underbrush. He ignored the clapping and hooting of her pack behind them as he chased after his sexy mate. Dusk had fallen, but his eyesight was good enough for him to follow Reggie's trail. He put on a burst of speed as the underbrush gave way to a soft, grassy mound a few minutes later and tackled the wolf in front of him. Reggie shifted from wolf to human as they rolled and landed with her juicy pussy right over his watering mouth.

He groaned and grabbed her by the waist, shoving his tongue into her tight, wet hole. Her shocked scream turned to a loud moan as she started to grind her pussy on his face. Sucking on her clit, he lapped at her, his fangs scraping against her skin.

Reggie threaded her hands through his hair, riding his face faster and faster until he felt her stiffen and cry out. As she shuddered over his face, he drew back and sank his fangs into his mate's tender inner thigh. She screamed even harder as her climax rolled over her again from his bite. A new wave of sweet juices rolled out of her tight pussy and onto his face as his reward. Isaiah groaned as he released her inner thigh and lapped at her still pulsating pussy.

"Isaiah, holy fuck. I need you inside me. Please, fuck me. Let me mark you," Reggie whimpered, and he smiled. Giving her clit a soft kiss, he rolled them over and crawled over her lush body, kissing and nipping his way up her stomach and side until he reached her heaving breasts.

"Fuck," Isaiah breathed as he took one of her hard nipples in his mouth. He teased her other breast with his fingers and she squirmed underneath him, nails biting into his back under his open flannel shirt.

His sweet bayou wolf arched her back, grinding her pussy into his painfully hard erection. Isaiah dragged a fang over her nipple as his mate whimpered and wrapped her strong legs around his waist.

"Isaiah, please... please... bury your fucking cock inside of me."

He groaned and reached down, releasing his erection and managing to shove his borrowed jeans off. It wasn't graceful, but neither of them cared as he aligned the head of his cock up with Reggie's dripping pussy. They both groaned as he pushed into her, all the way to the hilt with one hard thrust. Her pussy tightened around him as he started fucking her with long, powerful thrusts.

Reggie's loud cries of bliss echoed through the dusky dark bayou, her nails sinking into his shoulders. She turned her head, and Isaiah rutted into her even harder as he felt her teeth graze over his pulse. Biting down, she marked him just like he had done moments before. He felt his orgasm build as the sound of fireworks echoed overhead. Isaiah rolled them over, and they both stared at the sky with grins on their faces, watching the blue, red, purple, and gold sparkles dance across the sky. The new position gave Reggie the ability to take over, and she rolled her hips, her sweet pussy gliding over his cock in a relentless rhythm. He grabbed her hips and sat up, the new position hitting her even deeper. The root of his cock ground into her clit, and Reggie whimpered against his mouth as her pussy grew unbearably tight. He kissed her as they both exploded at the same time. Isaiah's cock buried deep inside while her silky pussy pulsated around him.

Breaking the tender kiss at the height of their orgasm, they glanced up at the sky as the last of the fireworks burst overhead. The colors danced across Reggie's skin, reflecting from her eyes as she caught his gaze. She peppered his lips with soft kisses, and they laid back down on the grassy knoll, his cock still semi hard inside of her.

He never wanted to leave this state of bliss, and he smiled as Reggie snuggled her face into the crook of his neck. She kissed the mating mark she had placed on him. "This was one hell of a homecoming, and the best Fourth of July I could ever wish for."

Isaiah smiled at her whispered words. "Then let's make it a tradition. Every Fourth of July until the end of our days, I will chase you to this grassy mound and fuck your brains out."

Reggie giggled and shifted her hips, feeling Isaiah's cock harden once more. "Speaking of fucking my brains out, are you ready for round two, my mate?"

Isaiah nodded and grinned before rolling them over. He ended up behind her, his hands kneading her soft ass. Reggie groaned, taking his cock on all fours as he slowly pumped in and out of her.

Shimmering silver stars replaced the fireworks as the sounds of the bayou and their soft cries of ecstasy filled the air. Isaiah groaned as his sweet mate cried out and reached around to cup her breasts. The position pulled her deeper onto his cock and he started to grind into her, relishing the sweet whimpers filling the air.

"Fuck, I'm coming... I'm coming," Reggie cried out as her pussy once again tightened around his cock.

Isaiah wasn't far behind, his cock twitching deep inside of her a few moments later.

They both collapsed, and Isaiah placed a soft kiss on her neck before pulling out and rolling them into the perfect star gazing position. Reggie snuggled into his side, her fingers roaming over his abs and chest.

"Yes," she murmured. "I think we definitely will make this a yearly tradition."

Isaiah chuckled and kissed her on the forehead. "I'm so happy I found you."

Reggie giggled and kissed his jaw. "To many more wonderful Fourth of Julys with the hottest mate a woman could wish for."

"I love you, my bayou wolf. And I am looking forward to a lifetime discovering everything about you."

Reggie giggled and kissed him again. "Me too. I love you too, my perfect mate."

The End

Snowflakes and Vampire Kisses

Holidays After Dark

Astrid Vail

Blurb & Content Warning

Decorations. Check.
Food. Check
Tree...
Damn, she knew she forgot something.
Ebony knows she is in big trouble.
Finding a tree so late in the holiday season that
won't cost her a fortune is impossible.
Unless she goes up into the mountain pass where
the *others* live.
Vampires, shifters, fae, *oh my*.
As a human Ebony was always taught to be wary of
the *others*.
Add into the mix a growing snowstorm on the
horizon and she should forget all about the tree.
But she would rather risk her safety than her
family's wrath by messing up Christmas in the
slightest.

HOLIDAYS AFTER DARK

***

The last thing Alexander wants to do is go out searching for a lost city girl, who may or not be looking for his tree farm.

He would rather sip blood and strum his guitar next to the fireplace, waiting out the storm.

Yet, upon seeing an SUV buried in a snow embankment, all grumpy thoughts leave his mind as he rescues the city girl in distress.

When her delicious scent hits him, he knows exactly who this woman is.

She is his mate, and he will do everything in his power to keep her warm and safe.

Good thing this snowstorm is only going to worsen.

Because she is going to need a place to stay,

And he knows just the place.

Content Warning includes adult language, on page sex scenes, strained parental situations (FMC)

Chapter One

EBONY

"RIGHT." EBONY GRABBED THE list in front of her. "Food prep, check. Clean house, check. Stock up on *ALL* the wine, double check."

She glanced around her small kitchen and into the living room of her modest two-bedroom apartment. The glittering decorations, strings of lights, and so much tinsel she was sure an elf threw up in her place, assaulted her eyes. "Decorate the house and tree, one trillion checks," she muttered to herself before crumpling up her list and throwing it into the trash.

The pop of the wine bottle opening was music to her ears, and she poured herself a great big glass. She one hundred percent deserved it after the day she'd spent setting everything up. It was the day before Christmas Eve, and she knew it was going to be hell for the next few days. Tomorrow, her family was visiting, and they expected her to do everything on such short notice. Which included picking them up from the airport and all the cooking for Christmas Eve dinner and Christmas Day breakfast.

Ebony rolled her eyes and put the glass to her lips, ready to take a big swig, as her phone buzzed. Putting her glass down with a sigh, she checked the screen.

> **Ebony!**

> **Mom wanted to remind you that you had better have a real tree.**

> **We hate those fake things.**

She sputtered and glanced up at the beautiful two-hundred-dollar tree she had painstakingly decorated. It was full, and enchanting, with frosted snow-tipped ends... And it was also one hundred percent fake.

"You have got to be fucking kidding me!" Ebony shouted to herself and scrolled through the email she had gotten last week.

She read the email over, painstakingly so when she had first gotten it, informing her of her family's impromptu visit over Christmas at her place instead of their typical tropical getaway.

Having followed the instructions to a T, nothing ever mentioned a real tree. With a groan, Ebony closed the email and got up, pouring the wine back into the bottle before answering her stepsister's text.

No worries!

I've got us a really special tree.

Show me!!!

Pictures now.

It's a surprise.

Ebony waited for her sister's response, and when nothing came, she blew out a sharp sigh of relief. "Fuck, where am I supposed to get a Christmas tree on such short notice?" She clicked open her banking app on her phone and winced. "Where *am I* going to get a beautiful Christmas tree, on such short notice, with a *very* small budget?"

With a shake of her head, she took a deep breath and opened the search engine on her phone.

Thirty minutes later, Ebony was ready to sell everything she owned, get plastic surgery to change her face, and move to another country. Of the five places she had called, no one could get her what she needed on such short notice in her price budget.

And disappointing her family was not an option. It didn't matter if everything else was perfect; one small mistake and this would turn from a walking-on-eggshells type of visit to a check-into-a-mental-hospital type of visit.

But she was determined to find a tree and wasn't ready to give up yet. She scrolled through her phone some more and, with another weighted sigh, increased her search radius.

Ebony felt her hope plummet second by second until she finally found a possibility. It would be a two-hour drive, but that wasn't what made her pause. The tree farm was over the pass, the pass that separated humans from the *others*. While there were treaties in place, and humans openly mingled with the *others*, Ebony lived in a human-only city. She hadn't been brave enough to venture over the pass and into the mountains ever since moving here, though she had always been curious. She hit the call button after another moment of hesitation, and a bubbly voice answered three rings later.

"Winter Haven Tree Farm, this is Honey."

"Umm...yes, hi Honey, my name is Ebony, and I was wondering how late you were open?"

"Hi Ebony, we are open until 4:30 p.m. Are you looking for anything in particular?"

Ebony glanced at the clock and felt her eyes water. "Oh, never mind then. I wouldn't be able to make it before you close. Have a great night."

"Wait! Are you still there?"

She nodded before remembering she was on the phone and drew a shaky breath. "Yes, I'm still here."

"How far out do you think you are?"

"About two hours. I'll be coming... I'll be coming from the city."

There was a brief pause before Honey's bubbly voice came back over the line. "We can stay open for you until you get here."

A blush touched her cheeks. "Oh no, I couldn't. You don't need to do that. Plus, I'm not even sure I can afford..."

"Oh, sweety," Honey cut her off. "Don't worry. Why don't you just drive up here and we will see what we can do, okay. It's not an inconvenience. And we don't hike up the price of our trees this close to Christmas like others do. We can get you something real nice for a good price."

Ebony choked on her words, barely managing a whispered *thank you,* and confirmed she would leave right now. She hung up the phone and wiped her eyes, brushing away tears of gratitude. Maybe, just maybe, she wasn't going to mess up this Christmas too badly for her family.

Grabbing her coat and purse, she shoved her feet into her winter boots before checking to make sure all the lights were off on the decorations. The last thing she needed was to come home to her apartment burnt to a crisp because of faulty

Christmas lights. Plus, she didn't need an even bigger electricity bill.

After shutting the door behind her, she carefully made her way to her small SUV, careful not to fall on the already slippery sidewalk. She glanced at the sky and the light dusting of snow falling around her. Here was hoping the storm wouldn't get any worse until she got back home with her Christmas tree.

Chapter Two

ALEXANDER

THE TRILLING OF HIS phone was faint as Alexander stomped his snow-covered boots onto the porch. "Who the hell is calling this late in the day?" he grumbled as he left a trail of snow through the living room to the kitchen. Service was spotty at best in the mountains when it came to cell phones, everyone and their mother knew this. Land line worked the best, no matter how antiquated they felt.

Alexander frowned when he saw the number flashing and answered, "Is there something wrong at the farm? Why haven't you closed yet?"

Winter Haven Tree Farm was his livelihood. Pristine acreage that Alexander bought and nourished back to its full glory after his required military service. And if anything happened to it, there would be hell to pay. He trusted his workers, though, mostly shifters and some fae, and knew they would fight tooth and claw to keep Winter Haven safe.

Honey's frantic voice clenched at his heart, but his worry about the tree farm dissipated with her first sentence.

"Nothing is wrong at the farm, Xander. It's just that I promised a girl from the city that we would stay open late to help her with getting a Christmas tree and she hasn't shown yet. I'm getting worried."

Alexander chuckled. "No need to worry, Honey. She probably flaked. You said the city? Was it a human?"

Honey paused. "I think so. But you didn't hear her on the phone. She was desperate and sad. I just don't think... No, I know she wouldn't flake."

Alexander pinched the bridge of his nose and took a deep breath. Honey meant well, she always did, but she took people at their word and tended to be taken advantage of. She also didn't spend a lot of time with humans. "Honey, I wouldn't worry about it. Just shut down for the night and —"

"No!" she interrupted, and Alexander was taken aback for a moment. Very rarely did Honey yell. She was sweet as honey, as was her namesake, but when her protective side came out, it was a shock even for those who had seen it firsthand before. "No," she said again, voice calmer. "Listen to me. I can feel it in my bones. Something is wrong. I can't reach her by phone. And I'm worried. My instincts are screaming at me. Plus, the storm. Xander, I think we need to go searching for her."

He sighed and glanced outside. It was snowing, coming down in big wet flakes, and it was only going to get worse over the next twenty-four hours. "Fine," Alexander huffed. "But you stay at the office. Just in case she shows; plus, like you said, the storm. It's going to get worse and, out of the two of us, I'm the one not affected by the cold. And call your mate so he knows why you aren't home yet."

"Thank you, thank you, thank you. Do call when you find her."

The phone went dead in his hand, and Alexander hung it up with more force than necessary. This was the last thing he wanted to do. He had planned to wait out the storm in his cabin, reading a good book and playing a bit of music. He just wanted to relax, but now he had to go find some city girl who probably turned around at the first sign of snow.

Forty minutes later, Alexander eased his truck onto a snowbank with a curse. There, sticking nose down, right off a side road, was an SUV. He wasn't sure if it was the girl's from the city, but he got out nonetheless to check the damage and see if the driver was around. The storm had turned for the worst earlier. Wet, flaky snow changing to hard pellets as the wind picked up. Alexander shielded his eyes against the assault, sliding down the bank to get to the vehicle. He knocked on the window and called out.

"Anyone in there?"

A meek yelp echoed, followed by a woman pressing her hand to the window, then her face. "Oh my god! Finally, a person. I've been trying to call with my phone, but there is no signal."

She opened the door abruptly, hitting Alexander square in the chest. The woman tumbled out of the SUV, taking them both down into the snow as she landed squarely on top of him. Grunting from the shock alone, he wrapped his arms instinctively around the woman.

That was when her scent hit him.

She smelled of chocolate, raspberries, and champagne. Decadent and mouthwatering.

His mind roared, fangs extending slightly as his darker nature rose to the surface. He fought his instincts, unable to both hear what the woman was babbling about as he fought the need to sink his fangs into her beautiful creamy neck.

As he struggled for control, the woman's pulse quickened, and the only sound reaching his was the rapid beating of her pulse. She became deathly still on top of him and, within a few deep breaths,

Alexander was able to wrestle his control into submission. The red haze that took over his vision disappeared, and he felt his fangs recede.

When his vision cleared, he looked at the woman's pale face, her dark curly hair tumbling around her features in a wild mane, clear hazel eyes wide with terror.

Shit.

He could taste her fear on the wind, the snow already beginning to layer over the top of them. He could only imagine what this woman was going through. Thinking she was saved, only to find herself in the arms of a monster.

"I'm... I'm sorry. You took me by surprise. I'm here to save you, I think."

Alexander's hoarse whisper seemed to do the trick, and the woman softened in his arms.

"You think?"

Her soft whisper stirred something low inside of him, and his arms tightened around her voluptuous body. He didn't want to let this stunning catastrophe out of his arms. Only when she shivered did he realize she must be freezing. He got up quickly, dragging her with him.

"Were you on your way to Winter Haven Tree Farm?"

She nodded, and Alexander took in the way her lips trembled, slightly blue. He cursed internally.

Taking a step back, her eyes searched his face, as if remembering he was dangerous.

"Honey sent me," he whispered and reached out, but not touching. "She was worried when you didn't make it."

"How do I know you're not lying?" she whimpered, wrapping her arms around herself.

Alexander dropped his hand and reached inside his coat pocket. He pulled out his SAT phone and punched in the number to the farm. Honey picked up in one ring.

"Xander, did you find her?"

"Ya, I found her. But I might have scared her. Can you tell her I'm safe?"

He gave the woman the phone and turned away to hide his smile as Honey gushed to the woman about how she was in safe hands now.

The woman cleared her throat a few seconds later and tapped him on the shoulder. He turned around, and she handed the phone back to him.

"Thank you for that," she chattered, shivering even more now. "A woman alone can't be too careful, you know. Stranger danger and all."

Alexander nodded and took her cold hands in his. "Come on, my truck is right up there. Let's get you warmed up."

Chapter Three

EBONY

STRANGER DANGER...

Ebony could have smacked herself over the head for uttering that childish phrase to the man—no, *vampire*—who just saved her from freezing to death. She smiled, trying to control her shivering as Alexander helped her walk up the snowbank and to his massive truck.

Which made sense because he was a massive vampire. Ebony wasn't exactly petite, averaging out at five-six and, as she liked to say, had a hearty appetite. But next to Alexander...

She spared him another glance, taking in his rugged features and strong build. He had to be close to six-five, and was built like a Viking. That was the only comparison she could think of, or maybe the stereotypical muscled lumberjack. Yup, she was just saved by a lumberjack vampire who looked like a Viking from a TV show. He even had pretty blue eyes.

Ebony snapped back to reality as she realized those pretty blue eyes were staring at her. She was just standing there next to the open truck door and looking at him. Crap, had he said something?

She cleared her throat. "I'm sorry, what?"

Alexander's lips twitched, as if he was trying to hold back a smile. "I asked if you needed help getting into the truck?"

Ebony glanced back at the truck and bit her lip. "Um, yes please." She held out her hand without looking, which meant she missed it when he bypassed her hand entirely, sweeping her up effortlessly around her waist. Her startled squeak echoed through the truck cab as she was gently deposited onto the seat, and her cheeks flushed when she heard his soft laugh right before shutting the truck door. She shook off her embarrassment and leaned forward, letting the warm air from the vents tickle her face. Ripping off her pathetic excuse for winter gloves, Ebony sighed when warmth seeped into her fingertips and throughout the rest of her body. She startled slightly as the driver's side door opened and closed a few moments later. Alexander readjusted the vents, so they all faced her way and turned the heat on full blast before reversing the truck back onto the main road. Or at least Ebony thought it was the main road. There was so much snow, she had no idea which way was up or down at this point.

"We can try for the small town at the base of the mountains. With this storm, it might take a while, though."

A long pause registered in the cab before she realized it was a question. "Oh! Uh, yes, the small town would be good, unless you think the storm is that bad. And in that case, is there anywhere closer?"

"Well, closer would be the tree farm, but it's just a small shack. And that wouldn't be adequate to spend the night in. Then there is..." Alexander paused before shaking his head and putting the truck in gear. "The town should be fine."

Ebony glanced his way as her vampire savior shook his head and removed his hat and gloves. He stared out the front windshield with unwavering focus, which gave her ample time to stare at him discreetly. She was spot on with her Viking comparison. He even had dark blond hair, shaved on the sides, and pulled up in a messy bun. She briefly wondered what it would be like to run her hands through his hair, to feel his strong, masculine body over hers. Then she snapped back to herself and drew in a long breath. She was such a creeper. Here was a nice gentleman, helping her out of a tough spot, and she was ogling him like a piece of meat.

A few minutes went by in uncomfortable silence, and with Ebony solely focused on her hands in front of the vents, she barely registered the truck slowing until it finally stopped. Jerking her head up in surprise, she spared a glance at Alexander until he cursed, and she finally gazed out the windshield.

"Oh," she whispered as she took in the massive tree laid down across the road. "That wasn't there earlier."

Alexander looked her way, brows furrowed, jaw somewhat tense. "Ya, I was wondering when that behemoth was going to fall."

A strained laugh huffed out of him, and Ebony bit her lip as he turned her way again. "I can't move that on my own. Contrary to popular belief, vampires don't have superhuman strength. I can try to cut my way through it with the tools I have in my truck, but the storm is going to make it difficult."

"Oh," Ebony whispered again, then mentally smacked herself. She was sounding like a doofus. She cleared her throat and tried once more. "Is there another way into town?"

Alexander nodded slightly. "Yes. Kind of, but we won't be getting there in this storm by truck. Maybe... Not to sound like too much of a creep, but would you like to wait out the night at my place?"

Ebony felt her cheeks warm at the thought of staying the night with this vampire. Her pulse quickened, and she squeezed her thighs together, glancing away to look anywhere else while he waited for her answer. Finally, she spared him a look and nodded. "Sure. I can do that if it isn't too much of a hassle."

He smiled, his face lighting up, and Ebony felt her pulse go into hyperspace once again. Then they were moving, Alexander shifting to gaze out the back window, the truck going slowly through the ever-worsening storm. The truck slipped, and she gasped, reaching for the handle above the door.

"Don't worry," Alexander murmured, "we will make it back in one piece." The truck straightened out under his guiding hand, and Ebony sighed in relief. She didn't need to get into two car accidents in one day.

Then suddenly, they were back where they started, and she saw that more than a few inches of snow covered up her slightly upended car. Ebony stayed quiet as he maneuvered his truck into a three-point turn. Once they were facing the other way, they started a slow crawl up the mountain. She adjusted herself slightly, finally relaxing a bit, and watched the snow fall. "I've never seen this much snow before."

"Mmmm, it's quite normal up here this time of the year. This storm alone is supposed to dump at least four feet tonight, maybe even more."

Ebony turned to him in surprise. "Really? That much?"

Alexander chuckled. "It does it every year. Did you just move to the area?"

"Kind of. I mean, I moved to the city last year. I've always wanted to get out and explore the mountains, but..."

Alexander glanced her way as Ebony fell silent. Twisting her gloves in her lap, she reached up to place her hands in front of the vents again. She wasn't cold anymore, but she was getting fidgety under her vampire rescuer's heated gaze. She jumped slightly when Alexander spoke again.

"You were scared?"

Ebony sighed. "Yes. No... more conflicted, I guess. I grew up in an all-human suburb and live in an all-human city. It's hard not to believe some things, even when you know people are just fear mongering."

"Humans tend to do that," Alexander breathed out his response. "Well, I promise not to bite.... Unless you ask nicely."

He chuckled, and Ebony blushed, laughing softly right alongside him. "Okay, okay. In that case, any chance I can ask a few burning questions?"

Alexander raised an eyebrow. "Go for it, snow angel. I'll answer what I can, and hopefully it will put you at ease."

Chapter Four

ALEXANDER

ALEXANDER HAD TO HIDE his smirk as the sexy woman next to him blushed once again. This time, at his use of a pet name. But he had to call her something because, in all her cute fumbling, she had yet to introduce herself. She twisted her gloves again in a nervous manner, trying to sneak glances at him under her eyelashes. He decided to give her a reprieve and focused solely on the white-out conditions and road in front of him. Technically, he didn't even know if they were still on the road, with the conditions being the worst he had ever seen in his time living up here. But Alexander didn't want to tell his beautiful snow angel that little tidbit. It was already hard enough for him to keep his hands off her. And he really didn't want to tell her why that was either, not until the right moment.

He waited patiently, driving slowly through the blizzard as his snow angel mulled over her thoughts. When she finally took a breath to speak, he almost sighed as her sweet voice carried over to him.

"So, this mountain. It's home to shifters and vampires, right? Who live here year-round?"

"And some of the forest fae. And a few human mates," Alexander added.

He watched her eyes widen. "Really?"

Alexander chuckled. "Really to what? What surprised you? The fae or the human mates?"

His snow angel blushed, and Alexander could honestly say it was something he would never tire of.

"The human mates part," she mumbled.

"Ahhhh, mates. Yes, humans are compatible to become our mates. We really aren't that different."

"Oh, oh no, I didn't mean to imply that." Her frantic tone filled the truck of his cab, and Alexander chuckled.

"I know, snow angel."

She went quiet for the next ten minutes, and Alexander gripped the wheel under his hands, hard. He wanted her to speak, so he could listen to her beautiful voice. But he wasn't the best at making small talk, and he didn't even know where to begin.

To his relief, she murmured a question quickly, without looking his way. "Can I ask you something personal?"

"Please do."

Glancing at her out of the corner of his eye, he watched her nervously fidget with her gloves. He wanted to put his hand over hers, to hold it and tell her everything was fine. He knew what she was fighting because he was fighting it himself. The only difference was that he knew why he felt this way and she didn't.

Instead, he left his hands tight around the steering wheel, waiting for her to speak.

"Do you have a mate?"

Alexander contemplated his next words seriously before answering. "I do."

His snow angel stiffened slightly, the scent of her emotions overtaking the air around them. She was relieved, but sad. Alexander almost spilled the secret right then and there, feeling remorse that he was holding back. But he was worried she might spook, and he really didn't want her to activate his prey drive if she bolted out of his truck.

"We are almost to my house."

He watched her twist those damn gloves again.

"Will your mate be home? Do you think they will mind that you brought me back to your house? I don't want to impose."

Alexander chuckled. "My mate isn't home yet, but she will be soon. And I don't think she will mind terribly."

She turned quickly, reaching out to put her hand on shoulder. "Wait, she is out in this weather? Why! Aren't you worried?"

Alexander could barely concentrate with her hand on him. He could hear the beating of her heart, the way her blood pounded through her veins, and he was doing everything he could to hold back his most primal side. He managed to grunt before turning around a bend and slowing his truck down in front of a log cabin. He hadn't left any lights on as he could see perfectly well in the dark and hadn't suspected he would be bringing anyone to his house. His snow angel pulled her hand away slowly, and the scent of fear and uncertainty filled the truck cab. Getting out quickly, Alexander let the icy air coat his lungs, and took an extra deep breath to calm himself down before opening the passenger side door.

His snow angel looked startled for a moment before giving him a hesitant smile. Reaching out, he helped her to the ground. She sank into the snow to her knees and shrieked. Before Alexander knew what he was doing, she was in his arms again.

Her beautiful hazel eyes widened in surprise, and Alexander chuckled before wading through the snow to the front porch. He didn't set her down until he opened his unlocked door and passed over the threshold into the foyer.

Flicking on the light, he couldn't stop his smile as his snow angel stilled, surprise decorating her face as she took in the open concept of his home. "Wow, this is... this is gorgeous."

"Thanks, here, let me help you with your coat and boots."

Alexander reached for her coat, helping her shrug it off to reveal a form fitting and light-colored sweater. He knelt, focusing solely on his snow angel's small feet and the inadequate snow boots she was wearing. "We are going to need to get you better boots," he muttered before catching himself.

Looking up quickly, he was happy to notice his snow angel hadn't heard a word he had said. Instead, she was scanning her surroundings, still in a state of awe. The man in him preened at the attention she was giving his living space. Feeling like a provider for her. His more primal state, though, was still roaring, wanting to feel more of her skin against his. It wanted to peel the layers of her clothes away one by one until he could sink his fangs and cock inside of his beautiful snow angel.

Jerking back from his wicked thoughts, he stood suddenly and tramped away, leaving chunks of snow from his boots. He didn't care that the floor and rugs would get wet. He needed to get as far away from his snow angel as he could.

Which at the moment was the fireplace.

He started loading logs and kindling into the massive thing until he heard the padding of feet.

Of course she followed him.

It was his home, and he wasn't acting like a good host.

His snow angel cleared her throat. "You didn't tell me your mate's name. I want to make sure I greet her properly when she gets back."

Alexander lit the match in his hand, pressing it gently against the dried moss, and blew on it until a spark caught. Only then did he turn around.

His eyes scanned the beauty before him as he blew out a sigh...

"She is home, snow angel. And she has yet to tell me her name."

Chapter Five

EBONY

"I'M SORRY...WHAT?"

Alexander took a tentative step toward her, taking her hands in his.

"You're my mate, snow angel."

Ebony blinked rapidly. She must have misheard the vampire in front of her. No, she really wasn't here. She had crashed her car, and this was some dream she was having while slowly freezing death.

"You can't... You...you can't be my... How do you know?"

She focused on the way his thumb rubbed at the back of her hand instead of looking at his face. He was much too handsome for her to concentrate properly. Definitely when her body felt like betraying her every moment it could. Right now, her body screamed at her to jump into this vampire's arms and let him do wicked, naughty things to her. Her brain, on the other hand, was trying to understand what this all meant. Or if this was really happening at all.

"Instinct," Alexander murmured. "From the second you fell on top of me, I knew you were my mate."

Ebony stared at him, unblinking, jaw slack, mouth slightly ajar. This was all too much to handle. She had been heading up the mountain to get a tree, dammit. Not fall hopelessly head over heels for a vampire, who claimed to be her mate. Though, to be fair, she had also been having some intense feelings the second she had landed on top of him too.

Ebony managed to make words come out of her mouth. "I think... I think I have been feeling the same thing."

Her eyes widened as her own words registered. Had she meant to say that? She was never this bold. "I... I... Oh, what is happening?"

Alexander chuckled and pulled her in closer. She let him, and it felt right. Everything just felt right, and she wanted to give in. She couldn't think of a reason not to either.

"What's your name, snow angel?" Alexander whispered again, snapping Ebony out of her shocked state.

"Oh! I'm uh... My name is Ebony."

She watched Alexander's eyes hood, his voice becoming thick with some unknown emotion. "Ebony, that is a perfect name for you, my mate."

She swallowed thickly. "Why... Why am I unable to think? I could think just fine in the truck, but now..."

By now there was no distance between them, Alexander having pulled her fully flush against his body. She wanted to tug at her clothes, feeling itchy in them. She also really, really wanted to know how Alexander's skin felt like pressed bare against hers. She didn't even know her hand was moving until it was in front of her. Her fingers skimmed over his throat, and she popped the first button of his flannel shirt.

A low rumble emanated from his chest, and he put his hand over hers. Only then did Ebony seem to snap back into herself, and her eyes grew wide. "Oh no, I'm sorry. I'm not usually...ever this forward."

She watched Alexander lean in, his mouth so close to hers. Her body desperately wanted him to close the distance, to take her in every way possible. Even her mind wasn't giving much resistance anymore.

When he spoke, Ebony focused on his lips, barely hearing him. "In the truck, you probably felt an attraction for me, but didn't know why. Now you know, and once you know who your mate is, your mind and body don't stop thinking about them. It becomes a type of torture, a violent need to have them at all costs."

"So, this, us, this is real? Not some weird vampire trick?"

Alexander shook his head, and Ebony heard herself moan low as his nose touched hers. He was so close, so very close, and all her inhibitions melted away. The only thing she could think of was him. "Can I trust you?" she asked, lifting her chin slightly, lining her lips up with his.

Alexander's breath was hot as he whispered back. "Always, until the end of time and beyond."

Bliss coursed through Ebony, electricity pulsing within her bloodstream as Alexander's soft lips touched hers and she sank into the kiss. It was absolute nirvana, and if she died right there in his arms, she wouldn't regret it for one second.

She opened her mouth slightly, and Alexander deepened the kiss. Her hands wandered up his chest on their own, gripping his shoulders. It felt like an out-of-body experience as Ebony was hoisted off the ground, her legs wrapping around his waist and her hands threading through his hair. She felt his hands on her ass, warm and strong through the thin material of her leggings. With a moan, her pussy throbbed, the friction between both their pants too much to bear. She needed to get out of these stifling clothes immediately.

Alexander broke the kiss, trailing his lips and fangs across her jaw and down her neck. Somewhere in the back of her mind, Ebony felt like she should have been alarmed that a vampire was dragging their fangs down her neck. But when Alexander pressed a featherlight kiss against her pounding pulse, that little voice disappeared altogether.

She tightened her hands, pulling at his hair. "I need you. Please."

The rumble that echoed from Alexander's chest made her pussy throb even harder, his hands on her ass squeezing. He moved, and suddenly Ebony had her back against the floor, resting upon the soft rug in front of the crackling fire. Alexander loomed over her, the buttons of his shirt completely undone, and Ebony reached up to drag her hands over the hard planes of his abs and chest. Leaning down again, he pressed his lips against hers before pulling away. He lifted the bottom of her shirt, pulling it over her head and throwing it across the room. Her face flushed as his hands teased the outline of her nipples through her bra. Ebony smirked as she remembered she was wearing a front clasping bra and, with courage she didn't know she had, she reached up and snapped the clasp open.

Alexander groaned, his hands cupping her bare breasts, and he flicked both her nipples with his thumbs at the same time. Ebony arched, the sensations seemingly flowing from her tits all the way down to her pussy.

"So beautiful, my snow angel," Alexander murmured before settling his weight down on her, and moved one of his hands, replacing it with his mouth.

Ebony gasped, arching into him as he sucked and pulled at her nipple, while his hand sneaked up to tangle into her hair. He moved to the other nipple just as his other hand snaked down to tease the waistband of her leggings.

She arched into him as his hand slid into her leggings, fingers finding her wet entrance. The throbbing in her pussy became unbearable, and Ebony cried out in pleasure as an orgasm rolled over her.

Chapter Six

ALEXANDER

ALEXANDER GLANCED UP IN time to see Ebony throw her head back, gasping and moaning as her first orgasm took over. With a grin, he placed a chaste kiss on her neck. "That's my beautiful snow angel. My mate."

Ebony sank her nails into his shoulders and moaned again as he continued to tease her pussy. His fingers circled her wet entrance, but he didn't dip inside of her yet. Inhaling her scent, he let his tongue dart out, licking her neck. His mate arched her back, her breasts pressing against his chest, and this time Alexander groaned. His jaw ached, his fangs fully extending as he scraped them lightly against his mate's neck again. The sound of her blood pumping through her veins was deafening, and Alexander knew he wouldn't last any longer.

"Snow angel, I am going to bite you. Now would be the time to stop me because, once this starts, there is no turning back," he growled and stilled, fingers and fangs poised to penetrate. But he had to wait. He had to wait until his mate gave him full consent.

His mate dragged her nails across his shoulders and up the back of his neck until she fisted his hair in her hands. She tugged at him, forcing Alexander to meet her gaze. Her eyes widened slightly, and he could only imagine what type of monster his mate saw staring back at her. Red irises, black veins running under his eyes, and lord help him, his gleaming fangs. He heard her gulp before taking a deep breath. "Will it hurt?"

"Do you trust me, snow angel?" She nodded, and Alexander growled, "Say the words, Ebony. Tell your mate how much you want this."

"I want you," she whispered, and Alexander released a groan before kissing her deeply. Breaking the kiss, he moved and plunged his fangs into the side of her neck, at the same time pushing two fingers into her tight pussy. He moved his fingers inside of her, and Alexander felt her shudder, just as her pussy pulsated around his fingers.

"Fuck!" his snow angel screamed, squirming under him.

Her blood dripped as Alexander carefully retracted his fangs, and he licked his way down her neck as she writhed underneath him. He left his fingers inside her, milking out her orgasm for as long as he could. Kissing his way back up her neck to her lips, he kissed her again quickly. "How are you doing, snow angel?"

She met his eyes briefly, ecstasy showing clearly in her gaze. She panted, "Why... Why did you stop?"

Alexander grinned and removed his fingers. Sitting back on his heels, he tugged her leggings all the way down, and finally his mate was completely naked for him. He let his eyes roam down her luscious body and reached down to free himself from the confines of his jeans. His mate gasped, and he glanced at her to see she had sat up on her elbows.

"Do you like what you see?"

His mate nodded vigorously and reached a hand up to him. Alexander chuckled and kissed her fingertips slightly. "What did I tell you, my snow angel? Tell your mate how much you want him."

"I want you, Alexander. I want my mate and his gorgeous cock inside of me. Please."

Kissing her fingers again, he leaned over, grabbing his mate's thighs and wrapping them around his waist. The tip of his cock lined up perfectly with his mate's beautiful pussy, and he pushed in slightly.

"Yes, please. I need more." His mate lifted her hips, and Alexander sank into her tight pussy a few more inches.

When he paused, his snow angel growled, sinking her nails into his biceps. "If you don't sink that majestic cock into me right now, I'm gonna..."

She paused, and Alexander chuckled. Moving his hips, he pulled out an inch, and his mate whined low in her throat. "Tell me. Tell me what devious things you'll do to me if I don't give you the rest of my cock right now."

His mate narrowed her eyes. "I don't know, but I'm sure I can figure something out."

Chuckling, he decided to give his mate a little bit of a reprieve. He sank back into her a few more inches, almost to the halfway point. His mate's eyelids fluttered, and she tilted her head back as the sweetest moan he had ever heard echoed out of her. "I'll let you think then. Don't worry, we have all night."

She arched her back, not even bothering to look at him, and cupped her breasts. "Maybe I won't let you touch these, hmmm?"

Alexander's breath hitched as he watched his mate continue to play with her breasts. With a low growl, he sank into her fully. "You win. My cock is yours. Now let me play with your gorgeous tits, snow angel."

His mate arched into his touch as he replaced her hands with his, massaging her tits.

"Yes, yes. More," his mate groaned as he ground into her, the root of his cock bearing down on her clit.

"Mmmm, you know what, snow angel, I want to suck on these beautiful perky little nipples."

Without any warning, he moved, rolling both of them into a new position, and his mate let out a squeak, sinking even farther down on his cock as she straddled him. Alexander ran his hands up her back to tangle into her hair and pull her down. Her tits swung in front of his face perfectly, and he took a nipple into his mouth while massaging the other.

She began to move her hips, sliding up and down his cock, and he moved his hips to her rhythm. Her breath hitched, pussy tightening around his cock, until his mate screamed, "Alexander!"

Dropping his hands to her hips, his snow angel came on his cock, her sweet pussy rippling around him. He thrust into her a few more times, and his cock twitched deep inside of her, spilling and filling up his sweet mate's pussy with his own release.

As she lay over his chest, limp and satisfied, Alexander dragged his fingertips up and down her spine, listening to her rapid pulse slow back down to normal. "Mmmm," she moaned, and he reached up to move her hair away out of the way so he could see her face.

"What was that, sweet mate?"

His mate looked at him with sleepy eyes and a lazy smile, before rubbing her head against his chest and closing her eyes. Alexander smiled and continued caressing his mate's back until he felt his cock slip out of her sweet pussy. Gathering up his sleepy mate in his arms, he carried her to the bathroom and turned on the shower. She opened her eyes and wrapped her arms around his neck. "Shower?" she asked groggily.

"Just a short one, snow angel, and then we can go to sleep in a real bed. Now, get your sweet ass under that warm water and let your mate clean you up after getting you so dirty."

Chapter Seven

EBONY

THE SOFT MURMURS OF voices woke her, and Ebony yawned before bolting upright, clenching the sheets to her chest. She glanced around frantically, taking in the massive king-size bed she was lounging in, the floor-to-ceiling windows that made up one wall, and the porch they opened onto. The view was majestic, snow and trees for as far as she could see, and for a moment, all she could do was stare outside into the winter wonderland she had woken up to.

She slowly came back to herself as a tingle ran down her neck. Raising a hand, she touched her tender skin and, all of a sudden, she knew exactly where Alexander was, so much so, she could shut her eyes and just follow the gentle nudge in his direction.

Ebony blushed and pulled the covers up higher and inhaled. They smelled of Alexander. The comfort of protection against the snowy wonderland just outside.

She snorted and pulled the covers off, swinging her legs over the side of the bed. She hadn't been that great with words before, but that analogy was ridiculous, yet it was the only thing that came to mind. Besides the burning need to find her mate. Lucky for her, she knew exactly where he was.

Ebony reached the door and cracked it open before slamming it shut. She needed clothes. Frantically, she looked around, before noticing the bed had handles near the bottom, and she pulled out a drawer. A moment later, she was dressed in a much too big flannel that hit her mid-thigh and sleeves she rolled up halfway just so her hands could poke out. Pushing the hair out of her face, she stalked toward the door once more and towards the voices carrying down the hallway.

There wasn't much sneaking she could do, as the cabin was all one level and mostly an open floor plan. So, trying to act as confidently as she could, she stepped out into the living room and halted. She couldn't stop the blush from attacking her face as she raised her hand and waved at her mate and the two other people sitting with him.

"Hi," she squeaked.

Alexander was out of his chair within seconds, arms around her and giving her the sexiest kiss of her life.

Her blush intensified as Alexander broke the kiss and turned toward the two strangers in the room.

"Snow angel, this is Honey and her mate, Blitz."

Ebony reached out a hand to shake Honey's when she came forward, but was immediately enveloped into a hug. "My goodness, I am so happy you are alright. Then Alexander told us the most wonderful news this morning! You're his mate! I am so happy, I could burst."

Honey pulled away slightly, and Ebony's eyes grew wide as the beautiful woman before her wiped at the tears in her eyes. "Ummm... Thank you, I ... Are you alright?" she asked as Honey started crying more.

Her mate, Blitz, sighed and took her in her arms, rubbing her back. "She's fine. My mate tends to get overwhelmed and cry when she is extremely happy or excited. Don't worry, she will be right as rain in a few minutes."

Ebony glanced up at Alexander as he wrapped his arms around her waist. He dipped his head and whispered, "Sorry. Honey called this morning, and it kind of slipped out that we were mates. Then next thing I knew, Honey was here with Blitz, along with a basket of pastries and other assorted foods."

At the word *pastries*, Ebony's stomach rumbled, and Alexander chuckled in her ear. Honey had finally stopped crying and wiped her eyes with a big smile on her face. "Sorry about that. We just stopped by to drop off the food, but I hope we see each other again soon. I would love to take you on a tour of the town and the tree farm."

This time, Ebony took a step forward and gave Honey a hug. "I would love that."

After a few more minutes of goodbyes, Ebony and Alexander were alone, and she sniffed deeply. Her stomach rumbled again, and she followed her nose to the kitchen, Alexander trailing behind her.

"Wow," Ebony murmured as she took in the spread before them. Alexander was right; there really was a basket solely filled with a variety of pastries and an even bigger basket filled with fresh produce, cheeses, and dried goods. Reaching over, she grabbed a scone and bit into it. She moaned as her taste buds were graced with a heaping of chocolate. "So good," Ebony said through a bite and offered some to Alexander. "You want to taste this?"

Her mate chuckled and grinned slightly, the tip of a fang peeking out, and Ebony could have slapped herself.

"Oh, shit. Right... Wait, am I...?" She paused, not knowing how to ask if she was now going to turn into a vampire. To be fair, she didn't really know a lot about the others and the mechanics of how they came about.

Alexander laughed fully. "No, snow angel, you won't be turning into a vampire. We are born and live the same lifespan as humans. We just have better senses and survive off of blood. But technically, I can drink any type of liquids."

Ebony blushed. "Sorry. I wish I knew more. About you know... vampires, shifters, and other beings. Makes me feel like a bad mate."

Alexander shook his head and came around the kitchen counter. He wrapped his arms around her, and Ebony rested her head against his chest. "You have a lifetime to learn about me and the people on this mountain. And I have a lifetime to learn about you. In the meantime, though..."

Snagging the scone from her hand, he brought it to Ebony's lips. She took a bite and groaned again from the rich chocolate. Licking her lips, she caught her mate staring, and grinned.

"Do that again."

His voice had gone rough, and he was staring intently at her face—her lips, to be exact. "Do what?" she whispered and licked her lips again.

This time, the groan came from Alexander, and the next thing she knew, Ebony was sitting on the counter, legs spread on either side of her mate's hips. His lips were on hers, and she opened her mouth to let his tongue slide in.

She could feel her pussy warming by the second, growing wetter than she could ever imagine as Alexander's hard cock ground against her clit. When she moaned, he broke the kiss, eyes tinged red and his fangs fully erect.

Ebony cupped his face and leaned forward, kissing one of his fangs.

She giggled as Alexander's face turned a little shocked before he snapped out of it and a growl came from deep in his chest. "I think we should get back to learning about each other, in the bedroom, right this moment."

Ebony shoved the rest of the scone in her mouth and nodded vigorously as her mate scooped her off the kitchen counter and stalked to the bedroom. She threw her arms around his neck and settled into the feeling of her mate holding her.

A feeling she knew she would cherish for the rest of her life and then some.

Epilogue

EBONY ~ SEVEN MONTHS LATER

EBONY SAT ON THE back porch, soaking in the last
of the dying rays of summer in her new home.
She had officially moved in a few days ago, after
her lease on her apartment ran out. Though she
hadn't been back to her place, except a handful of
times since mating with Alexander. Once to pack
up all her belongings, and of course, to have one
of the most awkward Christmas dinners with her
dad, stepmom, and stepsister. It had started off with
complaints about the decorations and tree, and the
weather, but then her mate had growled, effectively
shutting them all up. They hadn't bothered her
since, except for a short phone call here or there
from her father to check in.

Ebony shook her head and came back to
the present as she ogled her mate through her

sunglasses, loving the way his muscles moved as he brought down the ax on some stubborn firewood. It was just another thing she had learned about vampires after becoming mated to one. First off, the sunshine thing...total myth. Secondly, they don't sweat. Thirdly, vampires come in all shapes and sizes. Lucky for her, Ebony's mate loved keeping in shape.

He had removed his shirt some time ago, before Ebony had gotten home from grocery shopping. And you bet, the second she heard him chopping wood outside, those groceries were just tossed into the fridge, bag, and all, so she could stare at her mate. Which was one of her top favorite activities.

She lifted the bottle of wine to her lips, having swiped it from the counter on her way to the porch. She knew that he knew she was there watching him, but he didn't turn around. Instead, he put on a show for her, and Ebony was getting more aroused by the second. Finally, he buried the ax into the chopping block and turned around. His eyes caught hers, and Ebony swore she didn't take another breath until he reached her. Only then did she gasp and moan as his lips touched hers.

"Snow angel, did you enjoy the show?"

Ebony grinned and kissed him again, wrapping her arms around his neck as her mate picked her up in his strong arms.

"Tell your mate how much you want him," Alexander growled in her ear, and Ebony's stomach dipped, her pussy becoming unbearably wet.

"I want you and your cock more than I want chocolate."

Her mate laughed as he opened the glass door that led to their bedroom and placed her on the edge of the bed. Ebony licked her lips as her mate slowly unzipped his jeans and shimmied them off. Eyeing the outline of his massive cock in his tight boxers, she pulled up her sundress to her upper thighs and spread her legs. His chest hitched, and he took a deep breath as the thin spaghetti strap fell from her shoulder.

His cock was so close, close enough for her to just lean forward and lick it if she wanted. And she almost did, but she wanted to play their little game first. "Why don't you tell your snow angel how much you want her?" she purred as Alexander towered over her.

The growl from his chest rumbled through the room, his fangs extending and eyes going red.

The first time she had seen him go all vampire on her, she was somewhat terrified. Now it just turned her on.

Alexander took a deep breath, and a slow grin crawled across his lips. "How about I show her?"

Dropping to his knees, he hooked her legs over his shoulders. Ebony shivered as his fangs grazed over her inner thighs and his tongue darted out, teasing her wet entrance.

A low moan erupted out of her throat as she laid down against the bed and her eyes rolled to the back of her head. Her mate started off slow, licking and teasing until she started gasping and wiggling against his face. Then he picked up speed, thrusting in and out of her pussy with his tongue while he swirled his thumb over her clit. She came hard, screaming out his name, her legs clamping around his head.

Alexander pulled back and kissed her clit slightly before standing up and stripping out of his boxers. The bed dipped as he came over her, and Ebony smiled lazily as she placed her legs over his hips. He teased her entrance with his cock, pushing in slightly before stopping.

Ebony groaned and shifted her hips, needing more, but her mate stopped her with one hand. "Now, now, snow angel. Tell me how much you need this cock inside of you."

She arched her back and wiggled against him. "Please, just give me your cock. I need it."

Her mate moved, pushing in a little deeper, but Ebony knew he wasn't even at the halfway point. With a growl, she sank her nails into his shoulder. "Give me your cock, or else."

"Or else what, sweet mate?" Alexander murmured as he kissed his way across her breasts.

She moaned, arching into him as he made his way up past her collarbone to their mating mark on his neck. His fangs scraped against it, and Ebony's pussy clenched.

"I'll... I'll throw away all your shirts, and..." She sucked in a sharp breath as he slid his cock in another inch.

"And?"

"And I'll roll all the firewood down the hill and into the river."

Her mate chuckled and bit down at the same time as thrusting into her fully.

Ebony screamed as ecstasy flowed through her, pain and pleasure mixing into a euphoric blend as her mate moved his hips, thrusting long and hard into her aching pussy. Her orgasm consumed her body, sending shock waves throughout her entire system. "Alexander, fuck! Fuck, fuck, yes!" she screamed as he released his fangs from her neck and kissed her deeply. His thrusts became erratic, and all Ebony could do was hold on to him and let the pleasure continue rolling through her. She sobbed out in pleasure as he buried himself deep and stilled.

His cock twitched inside of her as her pussy continued its pulsating around him. Ebony gulped in breaths as her mate lay on top of her, kissing her softly along her neck and jaw. Threading his hand through her hair, he broke the kiss, eyes latching onto hers.

"I love you, snow angel."

Ebony giggled and rubbed her nose against his. "I love you too, my vampire lumberjack."

The End

Also by Astrid Vail

Wild Romance, Epic Adventure- Multi-Genre Romance writer
Mood Writing for Mood Readers
You can find my books at your favorite retailer and don't forget to visit me at www.astridvail.com
Wicked Fate, Lusty Mates

Carnal Moon: A Steamy M/F Paranormal Erotic Romance

Wild Moon: A Smoldering M/F Paranormal Erotic Romance

Enchanted Moon: A Second Chance M/F Paranormal Erotic Romance

Arctic Moon: A Sultry M/F Paranormal Erotic Romance

Feral Moon – A Seductive M/F Paranormal Erotic Romance

Scarlet Moon – A Spicy M/F Paranormal Erotic Romance

Fairytales After Dark

Claiming Jafar: A M/F Enemies to Lovers 'Villain gets the Girl' Fairytale

Gaston's Beast: An M/M Beauty and the Beast Retelling

Hunting Red: A F/F Red Riding Hood Reimagining

Princess Bound: A M/F Friends to Enemies to Lovers Second Chance Fairytale.

Wicked Snow: A 'Why Choose' Dark Romance Snow White Retelling

Holidays After Dark

Winter's Eve: A M/F Fantasy Holiday Short Story

Valentine's Arrow: A M/F Paranormal Holiday Short Story

Fireworks in the Bayou: A M/F Paranormal Holiday Short Story

Snowflakes and Vampire Kisses: A M/F Paranormal Holiday Short Story

Sugar and Spice Fantasy Romance

Violet Fields & Midnight Mountains: A M/F Cozy High Fantasy Romance

About the Author

Wild Romance, Epic Adventure - Multi Genre Romance Author

Growing up in the wilds of California, among the snow-topped mountains and stormy gray skies, my mind played on repeat, daydream after daydream.

Characters rooted so deep within my psyche, I could see them weaving tales of grand adventures and romance.

Bleeding from their world into mine.

Sirens singing seductive melodies while dragons flew overhead.

Courageous and wild woman fighting for their stories to be heard.

Villains shifting from the shadows to tell their tale, and heroes falling in love with the very ones they were meant to destroy.

As I grew up, these daydreams never left; instead growing into something more.

The words I write are the daydreams plucked from my head, inked onto paper for the world to see.

Characters with tragic pasts, new beginnings, epic love stories, and grand adventures.

Worlds filled with mythical creatures, urban cities, desolate landscapes, craggy mountain tops, supernatural beings, magic and, above all, romance.

Dark romance, light romance, sweet romance, and epic romance - stories where love conquers all.

Welcome to my daydreams brought to life.